9

MW00680878

GRIME AND PUNISHMENT (BOOK9)

A HARLEY AND DAVIDSON MYSTERY

LILIANA HART

LOUIS SCOTT

The Harley and Davidson Mystery Series
The Farmer's Slaughter
A Tisket a Casket
I Saw Mommy Killing Santa Claus
Get Your Murder Running
Deceased and Desist
Malice in Wonderland
Tequila Mockingbird
Gone With the Sin

CHAPTER ONE

Tuesday

January blew into Rusty Gun with brutal winds that had Texans everywhere scrambling to find heavy coats. The cold wouldn't last long, but it felt like an eternity to those who weren't used to it. However, the cold went unnoticed inside Grant's CPA office.

Deputy Jimmie James hooked his thumbs in his duty belt and rocked back on his heels as he stared down at the body of Leland Grant. There were going to be a lot of disappointed people come tax time.

"You want I should call the coroner's office to pick up the body, Sheriff?" James asked.

Coil nodded his head out of habit, and James flushed scarlet.

"Uhh," James said. "I meant Sheriff Davidson."

"You're right," Coil said, his face grim. "I don't belong here." He stood and moved to walk past them and Agatha reached out a hand to stop him.

"Coil," she said. But he left out the back door and shut it behind him.

"Let him go, Aggie," Hank said softly.

"Sorry, Sir," James said. "I didn't mean anything by it."

"It is what it is," Hank said. "It's the price of politics. Coil would want us to focus on the job and not his campaign. Or the troubles following him."

Leland Grant's office was an old three room house that had been remodeled and converted into office space. Walls had been knocked down so it was mostly one large area with an executive desk and two leather chairs in front. A leather couch rested against the wall, next to a table cluttered with Field and Stream magazines. The gas floor heater was lit, and the room was overly warm.

Leland had been the only CPA in Rusty Gun for the last thirty years.

"Excuse me?" Sergeant Joe Springer said. "Sheriff Davidson?"

Hank just barely kept himself from rolling his eyes. He hated being called Sheriff. As far as he was concerned, Coil was still the sheriff, but everyone had to follow protocol by the book or things could go south fast for Coil.

Springer might be Hank's least favorite person in all of Rusty Gun, which was saying something. He didn't think anyone could ever get under his skin more than Heather Cartwright, but Springer managed to take the top spot.

Springer wasn't exactly the quintessential image of someone who was chosen to protect and serve. He was slightly overweight, and his uniform always looked rumpled. His skin was pale and doughy with carrot-orange hair and freckles across the bridge of his nose. The chip on his shoulder was as wide as Texas with an attitude that made Hank want to give him a right cross square in the jaw.

"What?" Hank asked tersely.

Springer fidgeted from foot to foot. "Well, since I'm officially the highest ranking certified law enforcement official on scene, I think this should be my investigation."

There was a snort from Karl Johnson, and Jimmie James was staring intently at a speck of dust, shaking his head.

"And while I appreciate how you're filling in for Sheriff Coil," Springer said. "You are *just* filling in. And it's been a long time since you've been in the field."

Everyone in the room seemed to be holding their breath, and Hank felt his blood pressure skyrocket so he could feel the pulse pounding behind his eyes.

"Have you ever investigated a death?" Hank asked.

"No, Sir."

"Springer, have you even seen a dead body before?"

"Sergeant," he said.

"I beg your pardon?" Hank asked.

"You should address me as Sergeant Springer," he said, his face flaming red. "It's my rank."

"We're standing over a dead body, *Sergeant* Springer," Hank said. "Why don't you get the stick out of your—"

Agatha coughed loudly several times and pounded her chest, and Hank cut his eyes in her direction.

"—behind," he finished lamely. "So we can close this out and give the family of the victim some peace."

"I want this case," Springer said, stiffening his spine, and pointing his chin defiantly.

Hank had to hand it to him, it took some guts to stand up to someone as intimidating as Hank. That didn't make him like Springer any more, but it gave him something to think about. It also made him realize that even though he didn't want to be sheriff, he *was* the sheriff, at least until Coil came back. Unless he asserted his authority, the deputies under his command would run all over him.

Springer was being disrespectful and trying to assert his dominance at the same time.

"All right," Hank said, nodding. "*Sergeant* Springer wants to run point on this investigation. I'm going to let him."

"What?" James asked, sputtering.

"Well you heard Springer just like the rest of us," Hank said, looking at James as if he was a nitwit. "He told us plain as day he's the highest ranking real deputy on scene, and I'm clearly too much of a moron since I retired to know what the heck I'm doing. I should probably just mosey on back to the office and have some coffee and donuts and prop my feet up while the real cops handle things."

Springer drained of all color, and Hank nodded in approval. Maybe he wasn't as big of a fool as he originally thought.

"But Sheriff," Karl said. "This is Mr. Grant. Everybody loves him. This is no time to let Springer play cop."

"That's *Sergeant* Springer," Springer said.

"Up yours," Karl said, fists clinching at his sides.

"I'm writing you up for insubordination."

Karl snorted. "Yeah, right. That would actually require you to work, you fat lump of—"

"Enough," Hank barked. "Karl, he does have rank. Don't let me hear you be disrespectful again."

"Yes, Sir," Karl said through gritted teeth.

"Sergeant Springer," Hank said. "The case is yours."

"Thank you, Sheriff," he said, smirking.

"If you screw it up, you're fired," Hank said. "And since you're obviously more qualified than any of the rest of us to work this case, you can do it on your own. Let's go."

Hank didn't look to see if the others followed him outside and into the cold, but he could hear their footsteps shuffling behind him. He took a last look at a wide-eyed and panic stricken Springer just before he shut the door with a snap.

He tugged the collar of his wool coat up around his neck to ward off the wind, but the cold felt good against his face. Things had gotten a little too hot inside.

"Umm...Hank," Agatha said, and motioned for him to come to her so they were away from the others.

"Yes?" he asked, but he had a feeling he knew what was coming.

"What's wrong with you?" she asked. "There's a dead man in that building who deserves more respect than you teaching an idiot a life lesson by jeopardizing a possible murder investigation."

Hanks eyes narrowed. "You think Mr. Grant was murdered?"

"You taught me to start off with the assumption that a death is a murder until we're able to prove otherwise, or walk it backward to accidental or natural death."

"Good job," he said. "You were listening. I can get justice for Mr. Grant *and* teach an idiot a life lesson at the same time. If I don't assert my authority now, I won't have any of their respect while I hold down the job for Coil."

"So this was a test?" she asked, looking confused. "Men are weird."

Hank looked down at his watch. "Everyone needed a break from in there. Springer is going to have to learn what teamwork is. He doesn't have the skills or experience to tie his shoelaces on his own, much less run a murder investigation."

"How in the world did he become a Sergeant?" Agatha asked.

"That's a very good question," Hank said.

"I don't mean to interrupt, boss," Karl said. "But how long are we going to spend teaching that fool a lesson? It's cold out here."

Agatha rolled her eyes. "Good grief. Is there some man signal I missed since the rest of you knew what the heck was going on in there? Maybe if y'all would start thinking with what's between your ears instead of what's between your legs, things wouldn't get so heated so fast."

Hank snorted out a laugh, but it didn't last long. A frown marred his face and he stared at the team standing around him he was now supposed to lead.

"You're worried about Coil," Agatha said, picking up on his mood.

"Yeah, to say the least," he said, nodding.

"Me too," she said. "But Coil is a big boy, and you're the one who said he'd want us focused on Mr. Grant's death."

"You're right," he said, letting out a slow breath. His blood pressure was almost back to normal. "Let's go rescue the sergeant and figure out what happened to Mr. Grant."

Hank nodded to the others that they could go back inside, and he followed behind them. The heat had exacerbated the scent of death, and the smell clung to the inside of his nostrils and choked its way down his throat.

"Uh, Sheriff," Karl called out. "You probably want to get in here."

Something in Karl's voice had him hurrying to the area where they'd found the body.

All he could see was the soles of black police boots, the heels almost touching as they splayed out into a V. Sergeant Springer was passed out cold, his face paler than usual while beads of sweat clung to his upper lip.

"Good grief," Hank said, borrowing one of Agatha's favorite sayings.

"Should we wake him?" Karl asked.

"How about we throw him in a body bag?" James asked.

"I'll start digging the hole," Karl piped in, and the two of them started laughing, making jokes at Springer's expense.

Agatha knelt next to Springer and gently shook him, slapping him on the cheek a couple of times until he started to stir. Springer whined and curled into the fetal position.

"Come on, man," Hank said. "Have some self-respect."

Springer's eyes popped open and landed on Hank's. "Am I fired?"

"It depends on whether or not you did any damage to the scene," Hank answered. "We'll have a discussion about your future in law enforcement in my office tomorrow."

Springer nodded, and Karl reached down to help him to his feet.

"And don't worry, Springer," Hank said. "My entire career of working crime scenes came back to me in a flash while I was out in the alley. It looks like I'll be useful on this case after all."

CHAPTER TWO

Agatha watched Sergeant Springer's patrol car pass by and let out a sigh of relief. She didn't like confrontation. And if she were being honest, she didn't like seeing Hank in this position. He was different. Harder. Less compromising. He was unlike the Hank she'd come to know and love over the past couple of years. But she understood why he had to be that way.

Since she was being so honest with herself, she wasn't completely comfortable with her new role as acting detective. She and Hank had been working together and solving crimes, first in an unofficial capacity with the sheriff's office, and then as paid consultants. But pinning on the shield, even temporarily, was a bigger responsibility than she was ready to accept. She was a crime writer for Pete's sake. What was she doing standing over a fresh body? She had a book to finish and research to do.

"Umm, hello? Detective Harley?" James called out.

She had no idea how long he'd been trying to get her attention. She blew out a breath and tried to focus. She really needed Coil's suspension to be lifted. Stupid ethics violations.

"Right," she said, clapping her hands together. "Have you called the coroner yet?"

"I can do that now," James said. "By the time they get here, we'll have everything processed."

Agatha nodded and pulled a pair of Latex gloves out of her back pocket. Karl was already taking photographs of the body at every angle, but nothing up close yet. Death's reality was starting to weigh on her. She'd had training in forensics in her life before she decided to be a writer, and she'd solved real crimes previously. She could do this.

She approached Mr. Grant's body. He was elderly, probably close to seventy, but up until his death he'd been a vibrant member of the community. He and his wife had moved to Rusty Gun long before she'd been born, and they had grown children, though she couldn't remember how many. She had a tendency to hole up in her house and not get too involved in what was happening in the community, though all she had to do was ask her best friend Heather if she wanted an update on all the gossip. However, she couldn't remember any particularly juicy bits of gossip about the Grants. There must have been something, because Leland Grant had died a violent death.

The body was on the floor to the right side of the desk. The leather executive chair had toppled backward to the left of the desk. The carpet was old and worn in the main walkways, but it was difficult to see blood on the navy shag.

"Man, this place is stuck in the eighties," Agatha said. "Wood-panel walls and shag carpeting?"

"Men don't like change," Hank said. "They tend to stick with what they start with. Though if he's married I'm surprised his wife didn't make the changes for him. That's usually what it takes."

"Hmm," Agatha said, and then she whispered under her breath, "Good to know."

There was blood spatter across the front of Grant's blue Oxford shirt, and there were similar blood stains across his pressed khakis. One of his leather loafers was missing, and she scanned the area before she noticed it was wedged between a leg of the desk and his chair.

There was trauma to the side of his head, and it looked as if he'd struck the corner of his desk. There was blood and what looked like hair and flesh on the sharp edge.

"What do you think?" Hank asked.

"Misdirection spray," she said.

"My thought too," he said, nodding.

"What's misdirection spray?" Karl asked.

"Pretend the scene is undisturbed," Agatha said. "Mr. Grant is sitting at his desk doing whatever it is he does. Now look where the chair is compared the blood spatter on the front of his clothing compared to the blood and other DNA on the corner of the desk. It wasn't him hitting his head against the desk that killed him. There's high velocity spatter across the front of his clothes, and the only thing that could make that pattern is if he was struck by something hard and fast. The blood spatter traveled in the same direction as the weapon was swung."

"We need to find out if Grant had any enemies," Hank said. "I've only met him a couple of times, but he seemed friendly enough."

"Yeah, that's my impression too," she said. "He's a deacon at the Methodist church and he's a member of the Rotary Club. His wife is part of the Ladies' League, but she's not as involved in the community as her husband. She spends a lot of her time in Austin. I think they have a home there too."

Hank raised his brows at that. "I guess the CPA business does pretty well."

"No question about that," Agatha said. "They live outside the city limits on a big stretch of land in a farm house. Heather said she heard he was a real tightwad with his money, but everything they have is quality and well maintained. I was under the impression that was the reason Mrs. Grant spends so much time in Austin. I'm guessing things are a little upper scale there."

"That doesn't really leave us with a list of his enemies," James said.

"Actually, it does," Hank said. "We've got his entire client list. Money makes people do all kinds of crazy things. Seems like a good place to start. We just need a warrant."

"Too bad our IT whiz passed out cold," James said, chuckling.

Agatha rolled her eyes, and then took a couple of steps back so she could observe the room as a whole.

"What are you seeing?" Hank asked her.

"I think the killer came in through the back door," she said. "And maybe Grant didn't hear him approach at all. We won't know for sure until the coroner arrives and we can get the full picture for cause of death. But my gut says the killer swung from behind with enough force to crush Mr. Grant's skull. There's only one arc of blood spatter. Had the killer cocked back for another blow, I think there'd be blood on the ceiling or back across the center of this wall to the right of the desk."

Agatha swung her arms as if imitating one blow, and then cocked her arm back as if she was going to take another swing. She pointed with her other hand where the blood would've been flung across the ceiling and wall from the murder weapon if the killer struck more than once.

"What about the body position post-impact?" Hank asked.

She knew he'd already seen everything she had. Hank was brilliant when it came seeing what other people didn't see.

"He took the blow to the back of the head, and logically he should be slumped over the desk. But his foot was caught between the chair and the desk, so his body rebounded off the desk and that's when he hit the corner of the desk on his way down."

"Good work," Hank told her, and she let out a slow breath. "Why don't you guys finish processing the scene, and Agatha and I will head out to notify Mrs. Grant of her husband's death."

"That ought to be fun," Agatha said.

CHAPTER THREE

The Grant's home was about eight miles outside of Rusty Gun. Hank's initial records check showed that Leland and Evelyn Grant owned twenty acres in the unincorporated portion of Bell County. They had three grown kids and a smattering of grandchildren from the oldest two. Just the initial background check on property and other assets told Hank the Grants were worth a small fortune.

January in Texas didn't lend itself to beautiful scenery. The white rail fence that lined their property would've been breathtaking in the spring with green grass and horses in the pasture, but for now the grass was brown and the trees were bare, and the white farm house seemed lonely sitting in the middle of so much land.

The gated entrance was open, and Hank steered the BMW sedan along the winding driveway lined with naked trees until they came to a semi-circle drive in front of the house.

Agatha's hands were clasped together in a white-knuckled grasp. She was one of the most empathic and feeling people he'd ever known, but she put all of that energy into her books instead of into other people. It's why she had few close friends and stayed to herself for the most part. She felt deeply, and he feared if she truly let herself feel the depth of emotions he knew she'd suppressed through the years, she might eventually break.

Telling someone their loved one was dead never got easier, and that kind of raw grief clung to you long after you left the living behind. He reached over and squeezed her hands gently.

The house was rather plain—just a white farmhouse with a wraparound porch that had a swing at one end and a couple of rocking chairs at the other. There was a carport housing a Volvo wagon and a smaller car that was hidden beneath a canvas tarpaulin.

The porch light turned on, and Hank nudged Agatha. "She's watching from the window. Go ahead and get out so she can see you. It'll put her at ease to see another woman."

Mrs. Grant pushed open the screen door. "Agatha Harley, is that you, dear?"

"Yes, Mrs. Grant. It's me. Do you mind if we come in and speak to you for a few minutes?"

Mrs. Grant touched the pearls at her throat, curiosity etched on her unlined face. Hank knew from the background check that she was a good dozen years younger than her husband, and she carried her age well, but if he weren't mistaken, she'd had some work done. No one reached her age without showing some lines that only life could bring.

She was tall and slender, and her clothes were tailored and expensive. She wasn't dressed like a woman who was spending a leisurely day at home. She looked as if she was about to leave. Her hair was short, chic, and white, and her jewelry was tastefully expensive. She looked like she could give a snowman frostbite.

"I was just on my way out," she said, confirming his theory. "But I can spare a few minutes. I've heard you've made quite a name for yourself, Agatha," she said, ushering them inside. "Your mother would be truly proud, I'm sure."

Agatha thanked her and then they stopped and stared in the large foyer. Hank had never seen anything so white in his life. There was a complete absence of color—from the walls, to the carpets, to the furniture. The glare hurt his eyes.

"You can leave your shoes here at the door," she said before leading them into the front sitting room. "You didn't introduce me to your friend, Agatha, though I can deduce he's the man you're living with? There's been quite a lot of talk about that around town."

Agatha's cheeks pinked with embarrassment, and Hank took a step forward and extended his hand.

"I'm Sheriff Davidson, ma'am," he said. "We appreciate your time."

She reached up and touched her pearls again, and this time it was nervousness that came across her face instead of curiosity. She was starting to realize something might be wrong.

"Let's take a seat, Mrs. Grant," Agatha said, leading her to a chair, and then she sat on the loveseat adjacent to it. But she didn't let go of her hand.

Hank took the seat next to Agatha.

"What's this all about?" Mrs. Grant asked. "I'm really quite pressed for time."

"We're here about your husband," Hank told her.

"Leland?" she asked. "Well, he's still at the office. You should try him there. The next four months I'll hardly see him at all."

"I'm sorry to have to tell you that your husband is dead,"

15

LILIANA HART & LOUIS SCOTT

he said.

"What?" she asked, shaking her head. "No, you must be wrong. I'll just give him a call, and you'll see."

"I'm sorry," Agatha said. "We're sure, Mrs. Grant. He's gone."

The icy veneer vanished in an instant and she crumpled into Agatha's arms. Her sobs were silent, and then she looked up at Hank with tear-drenched eyes.

"How?" she demanded.

"We believe someone killed him."

"That's impossible," she said. "No one would hurt Leland. Everyone loved him."

"We're going to find out who did this to him," Hank said softly.

"I have to call the kids," she said. "They need to know."

"Are they close by?" Agatha asked.

"No," she said, shaking her head. "It'll take them some time to get here. My oldest is in Amarillo, my daughter is in Houston, and my baby is in Austin. Can you wait here with me? I don't want to be alone. What if the killer comes here?"

"I'll have an officer come out and sit at the house just as a precaution, but we've got no reason to think you're a target. Is there someone we can call for you until your kids arrive?"

"If you could call our pastor," she said. "He's a dear friend."

"I've got his number," Agatha said, getting up from the loveseat. "I'll call him for you."

Hank waited until Agatha was across the room before he spoke to Mrs. Grant again. "Did your husband have enemies?"

. . .

"No, of course not. I told you, everyone loved Leland. He was a good man."

She straightened her spine, and he recognized the look on her face. She needed someone to blame for what had happened to her husband, but there was something about her Hank didn't like. Her shock and grief seemed real, but he had a feeling she'd play the part of widow very well.

"Pastor's on his way," Agatha said, coming back to sit next to her.

"Thank you, dear," she said. "We'll need to make calls. Leland was very prominent in the community. This will affect everyone. Not to mention you've got a killer on the loose. This town has gone to hell in a hand basket. It's your duty to keep citizens safe, Sheriff."

Hank didn't bother to tell her he'd only been sheriff for a few days, and he didn't ask her if she was planning to run for office, because she sounded like she was reciting her platform.

"Yes, ma'am," Hank said. "That's why we need to get back to work on finding who did this. We don't believe this was random. A crime of this nature is usually committed by someone the victim knows personally. Maybe a client or someone else he did business with. Did he keep anything valuable in the office?"

She snorted delicately. "You must be joking. You did see this office, didn't you?" She shuddered as if Leland had committed the worst sort of offense because of his decorating sense. "He'd never let me set foot in there to help him. I always told him he could've been doing big city business if he'd just take it up a notch. Appearances mean a lot when business gets involved. No one wants to let a poor CPA do their taxes. It doesn't exactly scream of success."

"You said you were heading out just before we arrived," Hank said. "Do you need to cancel your plans?"

She twisted the large diamond on her finger around nervously and looked over his shoulder out the front window.

"I suppose so," she said. "I was waiting on my driver. It's Tuesday, and I always leave for my home on Tuesdays."

"Your home?" Hank asked.

"My home in Austin," she said. "I prefer city living, so I spend Tuesday through Friday there every week, and come back for the weekends so Leland and I can attend any events and Sunday service. Like I said, we rarely see each other this time of year anyway. But I usually leave before he gets home from work because Leland has never been fond of the arrangement. But I have to live my life, and Leland is at the age where he doesn't want to do anything but sit in front of the television when he gets home."

Hank raised his brow at that but of information, and he wondered if she had a backup husband waiting for her in Austin now that Leland was dead.

"You said you have a son in Austin?" Agatha asked.

"My youngest is still attending the University of Texas, so it's nice to be close to him if he needs me."

"I didn't realize Bud was still there," Agatha said. "Is he doing graduate work?"

Two bright spots of color appeared in her cheeks and she gave Agatha a look that dripped icicles. She was saved from giving an explanation by the knock at the door.

"Pastor Charles is here," Hank said, hoping to break the tension. Who knew her son was such a sensitive topic?

"Please let him in," Mrs. Grant said, as if she were talking to a servant. "I believe the two of you have delayed finding my husband's killer long enough."

CHAPTER FOUR

Wednesday

The "Re-Elect Sheriff Coil" campaign signs that had once lined Main Street were disappearing the closer voting day came. Even the sign once posted in the corner of the Kettle Café had been removed. Hank had a feeling that Coil's rival for sheriff was behind the backhanded campaigning, but there was no way to prove it that he could find.

Hank knew Coil was hurting, but he didn't know what to do for him other than let the system work. But he was glad Coil wasn't hiding away. The best thing he could do was be out and be seen as if nothing were wrong.

So when Coil called to meet for breakfast, Hank was happy to accept the invitation. As usual, he arrived before Coil and grabbed their favorite booth against the wall across from the service countertop. He ordered his usual of sweet tea and the sunrise platter.

Agatha was training for a marathon, so she'd left early that morning for a ten-mile run since the wind and dreary skies had cleared up. He'd been working out lately to make sure retirement didn't catch up with him, but the only way he'd be running anywhere was if someone were chasing him. Maybe not even then. He really hated to run.

He leaned his head back so it rested at the junction of the wall and the booth and closed his eyes. Coming out of retirement and jumping back into full-time police work was exhausting. He'd retired for a reason, and he missed working cases on his own time and whim.

He must have relaxed more than he realized because the next thing he heard was Coil calling his name.

"Morning, Sheriff," Coil said, chuckling.

Hank's eyes snapped open and he sat up in the booth, rubbing the stubble on his cheeks. Had he really dozed off?

"I was just resting my eyes," Hank said.

"Uh, huh," Coil said, grinning. "Is that drool on your shirt?"

Hank looked down at his shirt, horrified, and realized Coil was joking. Coil stretched out his long legs and propped an arm over the back of the booth.

"Please don't call me sheriff," Hank said. "I really hate it."

"Keeping up appearances, brother. You've got the title, and I wouldn't want anyone else to have it."

"Don't get used to it," Hank said. "I'm only keeping it warm for you."

Coil scoffed and signaled the waitress for his usual black coffee and pancake breakfast. "Hank, things aren't looking good."

"I thought your attorney was handling the appeal?"

"She is, but every time we make a move for information, someone in Belton puts a block on it. I know the allegations will get cleared up, but the plan is to keep stalling me until after the election."

Hank put his tea down without drinking, "Then why don't we drive over to Belton and figure out who's holding things up? Maybe teach them a lesson. I miss the old days of cop work."

Coil's mouth twitched, and they waited until the waitress set down Coil's coffee and breakfast and then went back to the kitchen before speaking again.

"You and I both know Oddie McElroy is behind this. He's got so many members of the ethics board under his thumb that even taking him out to the woodshed wouldn't make a difference."

"I still can't believe they've stooped so low," Hank said. "I'm not naïve, and I know how crooked politics can get, but this is a bit on the criminal side."

"Hank, welcome to the dark side of Texas politics. It isn't the norm, but it happens. I've stepped on a few too many toes since taking that oath of office, and memories run deep in the criminal underworld. If I was a betting man, I'd say Oddie was neck deep."

"How's McElroy connected to your undercover days with the Lone Star Rattlers?"

"Not sure, but that gang is deeply embedded throughout the state. They've been known to have political ties. And there's no telling who knows what and who owes who. Don't forget the millions of bucks in confederate gold we denied somebody. It wouldn't surprise me if there's a connection to Oddie somewhere in there."

Hank whistled beneath his breath. "That could be bad."

"Tell me about it. My past always seems to haunt me." Coil's mouth tightened in a grim line.

Hank felt for his friend. They all had scars from the job. He knew some of the details, but most of the information remained sealed in classified documents, and the rest was lost in Coil's memory.

"Maybe it won't haunt you if you bring some light to it," Hank said. "Not all of it. But parts of it. You need to clear your name."

Coil sipped his coffee and said, "There was more to that shootout than bad guys trying to put holes in me. It was a coordinated attack that began in a government official's office long before I crawled out of the dessert with half of my blood spilled along the way."

"Then why not expose everything and get it over with?" Hank asked. "As long as this stays in the dark, you'll never have peace to live your life the way God intended. Your family deserves that peace too."

"I wish I could do that," Coil said, blowing out a breath. "But my family is the first thing they'd go after."

"Who?" Hank demanded.

Coil clutched his napkin and wiped the corners of his mouth. Hank knew he was avoiding the question. It was killing him to see Coil in so much pain over something done to him for no other reason than his decision to uphold the law. Now the law was failing him.

"You know I can't—" Coil said, stopping midsentence as the waitress came back over.

"Let me give you a refill," she said, putting a fresh tea in front of Hank and refilling Coil's coffee cup.

"We appreciate it," Coil said, flashing a smile.

"Sorry to see you in all of this mess, Sheriff," she said. "But don't worry, I've heard through the grapevine Oddie has his own skeletons."

"We all do," Hank added.

"Well, you still got my vote," she said and bustled to the next table.

"See," Hank said. "Not everyone has turned their back on you. Don't give up this fight."

"I know," he agreed. "But there's more to all of this than just casting votes. This has been hard on my family. I'm not even sure Shelly wants me to continue."

Hank raised his brows at that. "If you really don't want to go through with this, then you need to make a decision. You've got people fighting for you, and it's not right to keep us in the ring if you've thrown in the towel." Hank wadded up a napkin and tossed it on the table. "We love you, and there's no judgment either way, but you have to want this more than we can want it for you."

There was a long, awkward silence. Hank didn't even notice the crowd noise in the Café. His head hoped Coil would fight for his position, but his heart wanted his friend to have peace.

"You okay?" Coil finally asked.

"Just tired," Hank said, yawning.

Coil yawned too. "Now cut that out. You've got me going now. The life of a sheriff ain't all glitz and glamour."

"Well, the life of a sheriff is cutting into my social life." And then he blew out a breath and dug for courage. "I'm thinking about popping the question next month, but I haven't had time to find a ring. Or make a plan."

Coil's face lit with pleasure. "Congratulations. It's about time."

"Agatha's been renting a room from me since November. Doesn't make sense to keep collecting rent, and I figured living with me might ease her into the idea. She can be stubborn. And opinionated."

Coil laughed out loud. "If you know that and you still want to marry her, then more power to you. I'm sure she's been a terrible roommate," Coil said, waggling his eyebrows.

LILIANA HART & LOUIS SCOTT

Hank felt color rush into his cheeks. He was too old to have a reaction like that. "There's been no hanky-panky. We're just roommates. And we both agreed from the start that we wanted to keep it old-fashioned. She's been paying rent, but I've been stashing it away for her engagement ring."

"You're going to buy your future bride an engagement ring with her own money?" Coil asked, wide-eyed.

"When you put it that way, maybe not. I'll figure out something. I want the ring and the place to be perfect."

"Then it will be," Coil said. "Now, what's up with Sergeant Springer?"

Hank didn't roll his eyes, but he wanted to. "What about him?"

"Heard he's looking for a job with the Travis County Sheriff."

Hank shrugged. "Maybe he'll be a better fit there. Or in another profession. Not everyone is cut out to be a cop."

"He's not a bad guy, Hank. He's just grown up in a bubble. He needs real world experience."

"Then he should join the military."

"Listen, this is where you need to take advantage of my experience and advice. You were like your own island before you retired. You worked alone for the most part, and you floated between the FBI and your local agency pretty freely. You didn't have to train men. You just told them what you wanted from them and if they didn't deliver they didn't work cases with you again. This is different. And not everyone is a big city cop. There are guys like Springer all over the country, and unless someone takes the time to mentor them, they'll either take their untapped potential away from policing, or they'll stay where they are and become horrible cops who help no one."

Hank sighed. "You're right. I'll take a little more time with him."

"Good," Coil said, nodding. "Now what's going on with the Leland Grant case?"

"Besides murder?"

"That was pretty obvious from the body."

"We didn't find a weapon," he said. "I'm guessing he took it with him because it had prints."

"I can't imagine someone going into Mr. Grant's office on a Tuesday morning with the intention of killing him. It looks like a meeting went sideways, and whoever was angry about it left, and then came back in through the back door to take a swing at him. Whatever it was they used to kill him had to have been something they owned, but nothing they wanted to discard."

Hank grunted. "I need more information on the widow. There's something strange there. And she's set to inherit a lot of assets."

"You get a chance to meet the college student?" Coil asked. "Talk about strange."

"Mr. University of Texas?" Hank asked. "No, but she was on her way to Austin before we interrupted her plans with the murder of her husband. He seems to be a touchy subject."

"Because he's the biggest loser you'll ever meet. He's been working on a Liberal Arts degree for seven years. But for all intents and purposes, he's a mama's boy, and the relationship with dad was strained at best."

"Really?" Hank asked. "That is interesting. Maybe we need to find out where Mr. Liberal Arts was yesterday. I wish you'd stayed on scene. We need all the help we can get."

"I hated to leave, but Jimmie James was right. I'm not the sheriff. Not yet, anyway."

Hank sat up straighter. "Does that mean you're going to fight for what's rightfully yours?"

"I'm done laying down and waiting to die," he said. "Oddie McElroy is going down."

CHAPTER FIVE

Agatha strolled through Hank's house with a hot towel wrapped around her aching neck, and a bottle of water in each hand. Ten miles of running had left her exhausted and chilled to the bone.

The roads had been so slick and icy over the last week that she hadn't been able to run without fear of falling on her behind. The sun had cleared things up, so she decided to make the run while she tried to process everything from the crime scene.

She was dying for a hot shower, but she was mostly anxious to discover what Hank and Coil had talked about at breakfast. Hank's text that he was heading home had made her hold off on the shower. Instead, she lit the fire pit out back and snuggled beneath a fuzzy blanket on the bench.

"Aggie," Hank called out.

"Out back," she replied.

Hank slipped through the sliding door with a bottle of water for her, and she smiled and lifted the two bottles she'd almost emptied. For having lived alone most of his adult life, she loved that Hank made it a point to be thoughtful.

They'd honored their promise to stick to their respective bedrooms, but Hank was always doing things for her in some way. She'd been independent for so many years, she wasn't used to having anyone—especially a man—be so considerate.

"For the sake of brevity," Agatha said, lifting the blanket for Hank so he could sit next to her, "I had a great run, I haven't showered yet, and I'm starving. So how did it go with Coil?"

"How about a hello?" he asked, teasingly.

She kissed him.

Hank raised a brow. "Talk about cutting to the chase."

Agatha elbowed him and he laughed. He'd started doing that more, and she loved to see it.

"Spill it," she said.

"Coil's got his hands full with the ethics violation. His attorney is on the case, but Oddie McElroy and his crooked cronies are making life difficult. Seems the plan is to keep him focused on fighting false allegations and out of office until election day."

"I'm not surprised," she said. "I love Coil, but his past and the connections he keeps make it hard to know what side of the law he's on."

Hank's eyes narrowed and his body stiffened. "Coil has always been on the up and up. I can't believe you still don't trust him."

"I didn't say I didn't trust him. I just said I can see how some people who don't know him like we do might have a hard time trusting him."

"I can't control what other people think, but I can be his friend."

"I'm his friend too, but let's face it, we're trying to solve a murder and salvage his career at the same time. We've got to pick one. Coil is a big boy. He's got an attorney, and he's got fight in him. But Leland Grant doesn't have anyone but us."

"You've got a good point," he sat back. "I guess we should get back to work."

"I'm going to shower," she said, coming to her feet. She reached down and took his hand to help him up.

"Coil has always been there for me," Hank said, putting his forehead against hers. "We go back a long way. There were times I didn't believe in myself, but Coil never once wavered. He'd call, and a few times he hopped on a plane and flew out to see me. We didn't have internet and Facetime like there is today. That never stopped him from being there for me. I will not abandon him, now or ever. He's my best friend."

"I understand," she whispered. "I'll always stand with him too."

"I know, and so does Coil. After all, weren't you the one who went to war with Dot Williams for talking trash about him?" Hank asked.

"And I'll do it again if she ever shows her ugly face in Rusty Gun."

Hank chuckled. "Good. We'll do what we can to support Coil. We can't let Oddie McElroy win. I need to run a background check on him. Coil thinks he's involved in shady business."

"Have you ever met him?" Agatha asked.

"Not yet," Hank said.

"You'll hate him. Come on, I'm excited about this case."

"You're excited about murder?" He asked.

"Well, not that Mr. Grant's dead," she snickered. "But I'm excited we're working together again."

"Aggie, we just solved a hundred-year-old cold case, and

arrested an FBI agent while returning millions of dollars back to the rightful owners."

"I know," Agatha said, "But we have an actual body to work with this time."

"Speaking of the victim, when's the autopsy?" he asked.

"This afternoon. Deputy James and I are attending."

"Do me a favor and bring Springer with you."

She gasped. "Seriously?"

"Yeah, I know, but he's young, and someone needs to teach him. He deserves to learn unless he proves he's unteachable, and the people he serves deserve better too."

Her lips twitched. "That sounds like something Coil would say."

"Everyone needs mentoring," Hank admitted. "Even me. Try your best to keep Springer from passing out during the autopsy. We're going to need him to get into Mr. Grant's computer. James secured the search warrant from the judge, so now it's a matter for the IT guru."

"How cool would that be if the killer's name is actually in the appointment book?" she asked.

"Kind of disappointing," Hank said. "Killers should be smarter. But they rarely ever are."

CHAPTER SIX

The Bell County Sheriff's Office was a small building at the end of Main Street. The city founders planned for there to be another row of businesses on the other side of the sheriff's office, but things didn't work out when Salado was chosen for the railroad line and depot. Not getting the railroad stifled Rusty Gun's growth, but not its character.

Hank sat behind Coil's desk. Coil had taken all of his personal belongings and photographs with him, but Hank hadn't bothered to move any of his personal belongings in. If everything went right, he wouldn't be there long anyway.

He shuffled a few reports on the empty desk, but he wasn't really paying attention. He kept checking the door to see if Agatha were there yet. He wanted to take another look at the report and photos from the crime scene. He could admit that his attention was splintered. Between Coil and trying to get ideas for his proposal to Agatha, he wasn't at his sharpest. Leland Grant deserved better.

He read the signed search warrant authorizing them to examine Mr. Grant's computer, making sure everything was in order. It wasn't as simple as looking through someone's home laptop. This was a business computer that contained financial records of almost everyone in Rusty Gun.

Looking in Grant's system was going to take a high level of discretion and confidentiality. Unfortunately, Sergeant Springer was their expert in computer forensics. He had a bachelor's degree in Computer Science from Texas A&M, and he'd been offered a good job in the industry. But he'd resisted the idea of moving to the big city for big pay and had bounced from one small police department to another.

Hank didn't trust him and he didn't like him. Springer was a know-it-all who rubbed Hank the wrong way on principle. Coil had been right, if this had been several years before when Hank was running the show, a guy like Springer never would have darkened his door.

The work he'd done was fast-paced, fast-thinking, and stupid mistakes weren't tolerated. There'd been too much at stake. A guy like Springer never would have crossed his path, but he knew Coil was right. Most of the world didn't operate at that level of excellence, and there was a learning curve. People had to gain experience from somewhere.

The words on the page blurred in front of him. Lord, he was tired. His mind kept circling back to Grant's appointment book. Would the killer have really made an appointment? Would it be under an assumed name? It was hard to hide anything in a town the size of Rusty Gun. Why hadn't the killer smashed the computer or taken it? He also thought it odd that a man Mr. Grant's age used a computer system for appointments. Hank made a note to find out if Grant had a receptionist or any outside help.

He heard the sound of boots shuffling across the floor and knew it was Springer before he saw his head pop in the doorway.

"Got a sec, Sheriff?"

"Sure, come on in."

Springer eased into the chair across from the desk, his shoulders hunched. He was a big man, the chair was just a tad small, and he looked pitiful. Hank had a feeling this was part of the Springer routine. Mentoring the man was one thing, but he had to do his part and take responsibility for his actions.

"What can I do for you?" Hank asked, removing his reading glasses.

"Sheriff—I mean, Coil, said I should come and speak with you about my future here."

Hank crossed his forearms tight across his chest. He might be in his fifth decade, but he was still an intimidating figure. He was built like a brawler, and since he'd started working out again, his chest, shoulders and biceps were imposing. He leaned back in the chair and raised his brows.

"I'm sorry," Springer said.

Those words were a surprise, but a pleasant one. He hadn't been sure Springer had it in him to humble himself.

"Can you elaborate?" Hank asked.

"I was wrong yesterday."

"And?"

"And, I'm sorry."

Hank let out a deep breath. He guessed that was all the elaboration he was going to get.

"Apology accepted," Hank said. "And if you're open to constructive criticism, I promise to help you become a better cop."

Springer inhaled quickly and sat up straight. "I'd appreciate it, Sheriff. Really. Thanks for not firing me."

"I've got a search warrant for Leland Grant's computer. The guys tell me computers are your area."

"You bet, Sheriff. When do I start?"

LILIANA HART & LOUIS SCOTT

"You'll have to fit it in this afternoon. You're going to be busy this morning."

"I am?" he asked.

"You're going to head out with James and Agatha to observe the autopsy."

Springer's face paled and then turned an interesting shade of green. He swallowed hard two or three times, and Hank wondered if he was going to pass out like he had the day before.

"You want to be a cop," Hank said, "You've got to figure out how to blank this stuff out. You're going to see things a heck of a lot worse than Leland Grant's body or an autopsy over the course of your career. You've got to go to that place in your mind where it doesn't affect you. And then you've got to find a way to process it when you're off duty."

He swallowed again and little beads of perspiration had gathered on his upper lip.

"Why don't you go get some coffee and figure out where that place in your mind is," Hank said, dismissing him.

He looked back down at the Grant report to give Springer the chance to escape, but his thoughts kept going back to Agatha. She'd been occupying his thoughts more and more lately. He loved her. He had fun with her. And he never thought he could see himself spending his life with anyone other than his wife. But he could with Agatha. It terrified and excited him all at the same time.

Agatha and Tammy couldn't have been more different, which he guessed was a good thing. His relationship with Agatha was...unique. His first marriage had been good, and he'd always treasure the years they'd had together, but what he and Agatha had was special. He'd be a fool to think otherwise. He couldn't describe the connection they had.

He only knew he'd been blessed with a second chance and he was going to take it

Valentine's Day was coming up, and if everything went right, he'd have a ring and all the other romantic junk that would make the moment perfect for Agatha.

"Hey boss, you got a second?" Deputy James said, poking his head into the office.

"Sure, what's up?"

"I ran back out to the crime scene to give it a second look."

"And?"

"And, found and lifted some metallic flakes from the desk chair."

Hank narrowed his eyes. "From the murder weapon?"

"Looks like it. It'll have to go to the FBI's lab for the level of analysis we need. That's way out of our league."

"I think I have a connection or two," Hank said dryly.

"I'll get it packaged and ready for overnight shipping."

"Good work," Hank said. "Oh, and don't give Springer too hard of a time at the autopsy today."

"If he faints, I'm not carrying him out of there," James said. "Are you trying to punish him or us?"

"I'm trying to build character," Hank said.

"Whose?" James asked.

Hank's mouth twitched. "That's yet to be seen. But good luck."

"What do we need good luck for?" Agatha asked.

"Springer at the autopsy," James said.

She scrunched her nose. "I'm not carrying him if he passes out again."

"You're both safe from carrying Springer," Hank said. "James was just telling me he found metallic flakes at the crime scene. Could be from the murder weapon. He's going to get them packaged so we can ship it to the FBI lab."

"Excellent," Agatha said, slapping James on the back. "Hopefully the coroner can find transfer materials in Mr. Grant's skull."

"Skull?" Springer asked, coming up behind them.

"It's that big lump sitting on your neck," James said. "We've all got one. Some bigger than others. Come on, Sarge. We'll get take out Chinese on the way."

Springer looked like he was going to started gagging, and Hank chuckled as they ambled out the door. Agatha gave him a wink over her shoulder, and his heart lightened. Maybe he shouldn't wait until February to ask her. Maybe he should do it much, much sooner.

CHAPTER SEVEN

The weather Wednesday night turned nasty, with freezing rain and blistering winds. Any chance of ice on the roads made drivers insane, and all of his deputies were out working crashes. The sand trucks were out in full force, and all the businesses closed early. Being from Pennsylvania, where they had real winter, the precautions blew his mind.

He'd been so busy with the storm that he hadn't realized Agatha, Springer, and James hadn't made it back from the coroner's office yet. A flash of worry spread through him just as the bell jangled over the front door and the three of them walked in, bundled up in scarves and sheriff's office wool caps in an unflattering shade of green.

Agatha unwrapped herself and hung her damp things on the umbrella stand in the corner. Her boots were wet and muddy and her cheeks were flushed red. She looked like she could still be in school, and he was reminded, not for the first time, of the age difference between them. It was something that had bothered him at first, but he'd realized quickly he was going to have to get over it.

"You'd think the three of you had been out in the

tundra," Hank said, coming into the open area to meet them. He'd spent too much time behind his desk and he was stiff. "Y'all need thicker blood."

Agatha rolled her eyes. "As far as I'm concerned, this is the tundra. I don't know how you're wearing a short-sleeved shirt. Unless you just like to show off your muscles."

Hank's lips twitched. "That's just a bonus. This is perfect weather."

"Remind me to never live in the North," Agatha said. "This Texas girl needs flip-flops."

"So noted," Hank said.

"How busy has it been?" James asked. "We passed Rodriguez and Johnson working a crash on the way back."

"It's been non-stop," Hank said. "I've been fielding phone calls about power outages and blocked roads. I went ahead and implemented a curfew, but I've got every available deputy out trying to get people off the roads and back home safely. I never thought I'd say it, but shutting everything down is the best way to go. You people do not know how to drive in this stuff."

"You're one of us now, Sheriff," James said, grinning. "You've probably lost your touch."

Hank grunted and remembered the close call he'd had a couple of hours earlier when he'd decided to drive around to check the roads.

"How'd the autopsy go?" he asked, nodding at Springer, who hadn't said a word since they'd come inside. He was still wrapped in his coat.

James slapped Springer on the back. "He did great. He turned a nice shade of green, but he didn't puke on the body and he didn't pass out. I call that a win."

"Good job, Springer," Hank said. "Do we have an official cause of death?"

"Blunt force trauma to the head," Agatha said, stifling a yawn.

James had a manila envelope in his hand and unearthed the contents on the counter. It contained photographs and copies of the diagrams the coroner had drawn. Hank noticed Springer looked away.

Agatha spread out the photos and then said, "The depressed skull fracture was comminuted with broken pieces of cranial bone displaced inwardly. The blow was so significant that it breached two of the eight bones that form the cranial portion of the skull. The force of impact ruptured underlying structures, including surrounding membranes, blood vessels, and brain."

"The blow also caused immediate concussion along with a laceration that tore through the epidermis and the meninges. Because the injury introduced an outside environment to the brain, the coroner classified it as a compound fracture. The coroner said as soon as the middle meningeal artery was severed, Mr. Grant was dead."

"That must've been one heck of a whack to the head," Hank whistled through his teeth.

"Yeah, that was the coroner's unofficial analysis," Agatha said. "Slivers of wood were also recovered from the area of the wound."

"Where he hit his head on the desk," Hank said.

"Bingo," she said, nodding. "But that would have only given him a mild concussion."

"Boss," James said. "If you look at the magnified areas of the wound, you can see a definite pattern in the unbroken skin. It may give us an idea of the kind of weapon the killer used.

"The pattern didn't look familiar to me," Agatha said. "Does it ring any bells with you?"

"It could be anything from a pipe to a parking meter for all I know," Hank said with a grimace. "But once we get a response from the FBI lab on the metallic flakes, it should clear up what the marks are. I called in a couple of favors, so we shouldn't have to wait too long for answers."

"Fingerprints haven't turned up anything so far," James said. "It's a slow process, but most of them are from the victim. Any oddities are partials or indistinguishable. Maybe we'll catch a break there."

"What's the word from the gossip mill?" Hank asked. He'd been a part of the community long enough to know that details spread like wildfire in the small town. Oftentimes things were exaggerated, but there was usually a kernel of truth in there somewhere.

"I talked to my mom earlier," Springer said, piping in for the first time. "She said everyone at the country club is still in shock. He was a good man and well liked."

"What about his wife?" Agatha asked.

Springer grimaced. "She's not so well-liked, but she's an intimidating force, so no one bucks against her too often."

"We still need to talk with Bud Grant," Hank said. "I was planning on driving back out to the Grant's, but the storm rolled in and created bedlam. We'll go out first thing in the morning, but let's run an initial check on him and see what his finances are like. Each of the kids might be entitled to a payout with daddy gone. And from what I've heard, Bud doesn't seem like the type who plans to work for a living."

"I'll do it, Sheriff," Springer volunteered. "I'm going to stick around and then sleep at my parent's tonight in case they need help. They live just around the corner."

"Sounds like a plan," Hank said. "See everyone in the morning." Then he whispered to Agatha. "I got us takeout from the Taco and Waffle before they closed down for the night."

"You're so resourceful," Agatha said, batting her eyes. "It's just one of the many things I love about you."

"You're not fooling me," he said. "You just love tacos."

CHAPTER EIGHT

Thursday

Hank woke early the next morning. The fact that his brain had never really turned off during the night had led to restless sleep, and he figured he was better off up and checking on his deputies than tossing and turning in bed.

The wind whipped and howled against the windows, and he stood in the kitchen, looking out the sliding glass door and into the back yard. He had his usual breakfast—a banana and Ensure—and wished he'd put on a pair of socks. The travertine tile was freezing beneath his bare feet.

"You sure do think loud," Agatha said from behind him.

"You're up early," he said, leaning down to give her a kiss. She grunted and went to the coffeemaker, and he hid a grin. Agatha was not a sociable morning person, which is why she chose to run first thing every morning. It gave her time to wake up. The days she couldn't run—well, those days were best approached like poking a lion with a stick.

She'd left the door to her bedroom open, and he was still amazed with what she'd managed to do with the space that had previously been nothing but four white walls. He'd wanted her to feel at home, and he'd already had some remodels in mind when he'd bought the house a couple of years before. But he wanted Agatha to have input too.

She still treated it like it was his house, and she was only a tenant. But he didn't want her to feel that way at all. He wanted this to be *their* home.

"Do you mind if I go with you to talk to Bud Grant?" she asked, squinting at the button on the coffee maker.

"Sure," he said. "I've already called in to check on the roads. There are a couple of icy spots in higher elevated areas, but the ground is still too warm for them to be too bad. Schools and businesses are all going to open a couple of hours late."

"Good," she said. "Let's take my Jeep. The roads heading out to the Grant place will be pretty muddy."

Hank grunted in assent.

"Springer texted a few minutes ago," she said once she'd taken the first sip of coffee.

Hank watched the life slowly seep into her until her eyes were alert. "And what did Springer say?" he prompted.

"He's been up all night trying to get into Grant's computer."

"Any luck?"

"Not yet," she said.

An hour later they were both showered and dressed, and they quick-stepped through a chilly drizzle towards Agatha's Jeep Wrangler under the carport. That was the thing about old houses, they rarely came with a garage.

Springer had a productive night, because Hank found the background check he'd run on Bud Grant waiting for him in his email. He tried to occupy himself from Agatha's driving by reading Springer's email. It wasn't easy. He hated not being the one behind the wheel.

"Tell me about Bud Grant," she said, making a turn entirely too fast in his opinion.

"He's got a few speeding tickets, a drunk and disorderly, and a DUI under his belt, but all were dismissed. He was accused of rape at a frat party a few years ago, but it was hushed up and it looks like a settlement was made so charges weren't filed. Basically, it looks like his parent's money has kept him out of jail."

"I guess he doesn't learn from his mistakes," she said.

"Or he expects mommy to clean up the mess after him," Hank answered.

It was just after eight-thirty by the time the pulled into the U-shaped driveway. A woman came to the door Hank didn't recognize, but Agatha waved at her.

"Audrey Pierce," she said. "She's one of the country club regulars."

"And?" Hank asked.

"My mother always said to keep my mouth shut if I don't have anything nice to say about anyone."

Hank snorted and put the car in park. And then he and Agatha walked back to the front door of the farmhouse.

"Well, Agatha Harley," Audrey said, looking her over from head to toe disapprovingly. "It's been years since I've seen you. I don't think we travel in the same circles."

Audrey was a small, thin woman with black hair cut in a stylish bob. She had a streak of silver in the front, reminding him of Cruella de Vil, and her eyes had the kind of surprised wideness about them that only came with too much plastic surgery.

"No, ma'am," Agatha said at the slight.

"I've heard all about the little books you write," she went on. "Such a nice hobby."

He watched Agatha's jaw clench and was surprised at her restraint.

"It's much more than a hobby," Hank cut in. "She's one of the bestselling authors in the world."

Her gaze turned toward him and he arched a brow, daring her to say something else about Agatha.

"And who is this?" she asked, her eyes returning to Agatha. "Is this the new boyfriend? I'd heard you'd moved in together. What would your mother say about that, dear?"

"She'd say to do what's best for me and ignore the busybodies," Agatha said sweetly.

"I'm Sheriff Davidson," Hank broke in before the woman could retort. "We're here to speak with Bud Grant."

She straightened her spine and faced Hank square on. "Which is exactly why I'm here. To be the gatekeeper for the family. They've suffered a terrible loss, and they don't need harassment. They need you out there finding who did this. I'm sure the taxpayers would agree."

"I've never heard that one before," Hank said good-naturedly, though he had more than he could count.

"Evelyn and the children are all still sleeping. I'll make sure to give them the message that you paid a call when they wake up."

"No need," Hank said, his smile never leaving his face. "We don't need to see anyone but Bud. So maybe you can let him and the concerned taxpayers know that we'll speak to him here or down at the station."

Audrey's mouth dropped open in shock. "I beg your pardon?"

"We'll wait in here," Hank said, walking past her into the front parlor where they'd spoken with Mrs. Grant previously. Agatha followed him in and stood in front of the fireplace.

By the time Hank had turned around again Audrey was gone. Hopefully to get Bud.

"Holy cow," Agatha said. "I thought she was going to punch you."

"Nah, I was nice. Didn't you see my smile?"

"Yeah, just like before a shark eats it's prey," she said. "I don't think you can count on her vote."

"Good thing I'm not running for sheriff then."

They waited a good fifteen minutes before they heard someone coming down the stairs. And then Bud Grant stumbled into view in stained gray sweatpants and a thin white t-shirt, his thinning hair mussed and stubble thick on his face.

"I'm going to file a complaint," he said, coming in and falling onto the couch. "This is harassment."

"You're free to file a complaint," Hank said. "But you'll have a hard time convincing anyone of harassment since this is the first time we've spoken. Surely of all the classes you've taken through the years you learned something about the law."

"Whatever," Bud said. "What do you want?"

"We want to talk about your father," Hank said.

"Someone killed him," Bud said. "And you should be out there looking for the killer instead of rousting me."

"When did you get into town?" Hank asked.

"Yesterday," he said, shrugging.

"How'd you get here?" Hank asked. "I didn't see a car out front."

"I drive a little MG Roadster. Bright yellow. Can't miss it."

"Did you and your father get along?" Hank asked.

"Well enough," Bud said. "We mostly stayed out of each other's way. He was old and set in his ways, and we didn't really see eye to eye. He didn't really like doing much besides work. Sometimes he played golf."

"What was it you didn't see eye to eye about?"

Bud shrugged. "Life mostly. He thought I was wasting time and his money in school. He thought it was time I settle down and find a career. That kind of thing. Didn't matter. Mom always understood me better."

"When was the last time you and your father spoke?" Hank asked.

"I don't remember," he said. "It's been awhile."

"Thanks for your time," Hank said, coming to his feet. He could tell Bud was surprised by the abrupt departure. "We'll see ourselves out."

"That's what you woke me up for?" he asked, incredulously.

"Yep," Hank said, and gave him a smile that made him shrivel.

"He was lying about not knowing when the last time he spoke to his father was," Agatha said once they'd gotten back on the road. She took the corner slowly, remembering how slick the gravel and mud road had been on the way out.

"That's not all he was lying about," Hank said.

"The car?" she asked.

Hank nodded. "Exactly. Bud's a moron, and his parent's money has bought him out of every troubled situation he's ever been in. That MG Roadster was parked under the carport when we came to notify Mrs. Grant about her husband. So either Bud didn't drive it into town, or Mrs. Grant was lying when she said Bud was still in Austin."

"She's used to covering for him," Agatha said. "If she

had even a suspicion that Bud might have committed murder, it was probably second nature to lie and cover for him."

"Or she's in on it too," Hank said.

"If he's our killer, maybe he was dumb enough to leave the murder weapon in his car."

"I'm going to put James on this," Hank said. "We'll cook up something and then get Bud to come into town."

"How is that going to get us access to search his car?" Agatha asked.

"I noticed in the report Springer sent that the license plates are expired on his precious car. Makes sense to me that James would pull him over for the violation."

"Oh," Agatha said, a smile spreading across her face. "Makes perfect sense."

CHAPTER NINE

"Hey, Sheriff," Springer said when they finally made it back to the office. It had started to drizzle again, and the drive back had been slow.

"Springer," Hank said, nodding. "Anything new for us?"

He hung up his coat and then used the Keurig to make a cup of hot tea, then he put in coffee for Agatha.

"Yes, Sir," Springer said. "But we should take it into your office."

Hank nodded and handed Agatha her coffee, and then he closed the door of his office behind them.

"I finally got into Grant's files," Springer said excitedly. "I'm guessing he hired someone to input thirty years worth of files, because it's all in there. Honestly, some of the programs he has are pretty high tech. I'd be surprised if a guy his age was that tech savvy."

"I read in the file that he's got a receptionist that comes in three days a week," Hank said. "She was off the day he was killed, but James went to interview her. She didn't have access to his computer because of the sensitive data, but I'm sure she can tell us the name of the company he used."

"What about his appointment book?" Agatha asked. "And why didn't the receptionist keep his appointments?"

"She told James she tried to keep his calendar straight when she first started working there," Hank said. "But he kept making appointments with clients that he didn't want to put on the books. Apparently, some of his wealthier clients didn't want record of who handled their financials. So he'd make the appointments himself and leave her in the dark. So she gave up keeping the calendar. She comes in to pay bills, make postal runs, and run Interference with his regular clients if need be. She said it was an easy job."

Hank turned back to Springer. "Please tell me he kept his own appointment book on his personal computer."

Springer nodded. "Again, he used an outside company, and clients could call a number and a third party would set his schedule. It was all completely confidential, which I guess is why Grant preferred that rather than a receptionist who's liable to run her mouth at the salon. From what I could find, his everyday clients were coded in blue, and his special clients were coded in red. And he only saw his special clients on the days his receptionist didn't come into the office."

"Makes sense," Hank said. "Good work, Springer. Keep searching and let's see who these special clients are. I think whoever we're looking for, money is the name of the game. We need to know who's going to inherit what, and if any of his special clients have anything funny going on in their accounting. Payoffs, blackmail, money laundering, phony accounts."

"Yessir, Sheriff," Springer said.

"But what about Bud?" Agatha asked. "He lied to us for a reason. I thought he was our main suspect."

"He's definitely a suspect," Hank said. "Along with mama and anyone on that client list we can't rule out."

"Oh," Springer said, interrupting. "I've got information on Bud. Grant had a line item budget for his youngest son. Looks like a real piece of work."

"What do you mean?" Hank asked. "You didn't think that was important information?"

"I forgot about it until you said his name," Springer said. "I haven't been to bed yet."

"Right," Hank said. "What do you mean about a line item budget?"

"There were steady deposits going into Bud's account every month. I just added up the last year and it's well over my pay grade."

"Did he miss any payments?" Hank asked.

"How'd you know?" Springer asked.

"Intuition," Hank said.

Springer nodded. "The last payment was made two months ago."

"I guess things have been getting a little tight for Bud," Hank said, looking at Agatha.

"He'd be getting something from his mother," Agatha said. "She wouldn't let him go without."

"It's enough for a warrant to dig deep into Bud and Evelyn's personal finances. I'm going to assume Evelyn had her own accounts separate from her husband."

"I'd say that's accurate," Springer said. "Grant transferred money into an account for his wife every month as well."

"Okay," Hank said. "I'll contact the judge about the warrant. You keep working the files. We can't assume it's Bud or Evelyn just because the signs point that direction."

"You got it, Boss," Springer said. "Mr. Grant was a good

man. We've got to find who did this to him. He didn't just do work in the community. He was admired all over the state. He even served on the state board for finances. He had to make the occasional trip to Austin for meetings, but they had a house there."

Springer walked out and left them alone, and then he stuck his head back in. "Oh, yeah. You got a call from Oddie McElroy. Wants you to call him back."

"I can't imagine why," Hank said surprised.

"He needs cash," Springer said, laughing. "He wants you to make a donation to his campaign."

"Seriously?" Agatha said, gasping. "I'll give him a donation with my fist."

Hank chuckled. "He's just trying to get in our heads. I'll call him later to politely decline."

"Yeah," Springer said. "I didn't take you for much of a golfer anyway."

"Golfer?" Hank asked.

"He's hosting a fundraiser at the country club."

"It's the middle of January," Agatha said. "It's freezing."

"Real golfers don't care about the weather," Springer said. "And all those big-money people aren't going to be out on the golf course much anyway. They're going to be showing off for each other inside. Don't forget that's the world I came from."

"You'll make a good cop, Springer," Hank said. "You put that world in the past tense."

CHAPTER TEN

Hank picked up the old plastic receiver, and then put it back down again. He stared at the number on the pad in front of him, knowing it belonged to a man who'd never strapped on a shield or a weapon or sworn to serve and protect. He had to get his anger under control before he made the call. Anger gave the other person power.

Hank knew Oddie McElroy was only interested in serving himself, and it was obvious he'd do whatever it took to win the sheriff's election. Even if it cost Coil his reputation.

"Friends close," he said to himself. "Enemies closer."

He dialed and waited until someone picked up.

"McElroy," he slurred.

Hank raised his brows. The guy sounded drunk.

"Is this Oddie McElroy?" Hank asked.

"That's my name," he said. "Who's this?"

"This is Hank Davidson. I'm returning your call."

"That's right smart of you son," he said, cackling. "You know which side the bread is going to be buttered on. If you put your support behind me in the election, I've got a real special position for you. And it pays very well."

"I can't be bribed, Mr. McElroy," Hank said. "It was a mistake to return your call."

"I can end you, boy," McElroy said. "Better be careful how you talk to me."

"I don't know who you're calling boy, but I've spent a career dealing with people a lot worse than you. Don't threaten me. Ever."

"This ain't the big city, Davidson. You have no idea the viper's nest you'll step in if you oppose me."

"Consider yourself opposed," Hank said. "I've learned how to kill snakes." And then he hung up.

James stuck his head in the door a few minutes later. "We got a call from the FBI lab."

"What'd they say?"

"The metallic flakes recovered from the chair and collected from the tissue of the victim during the autopsy are a match."

"But they don't know what was used to kill the victim?"

"Bingo," James said.

Hank sighed. "Why can't it ever be easy?"

The sun came out after noon and the temperature rose to the forties, so Agatha took an hour to get in a run. It helped clear her head, and she could get her training in at the same time.

She showered and changed, and then headed back into town, hoping Hank was in the mood for lunch. She'd put on jeans and boots and a long-sleeve gray Henley under her jacket, and put her hair in a knot on her head.

The sheriff's office was empty when she came inside, so she went straight back to Hank's office.

"Hey Sheriff," she said, knocking on the doorframe. "Busy?"

Hank was massaging his temples, and he had that look he got when he was upset but didn't want anyone to notice.

"Am I busy?" he asked.

"I'm just messing with you," she said quickly. "I can tell you're overloaded."

"Have a good run?" Hank asked. He stood and gave her a quick hug.

"Yes. Very. I'm back with a clear head and empty stomach. I'm starving."

Hank chuckled. "I guess you want me to feed you?"

"I wouldn't turn it down," she said. "And maybe you can tell me what's wrong."

"I called Oddie McElroy back. It seems he thinks I can be bought by coming to the dark side. And the he gave me a veiled threat about not picking the right team. I'm half tempted to go throw cuffs on him."

"I'm sorry he got under your skin," she said. "Maybe he'll do something stupid and you'll get to arrest him after all."

"I don't want to talk about McElroy anymore," Hank said. "He's ruining my appetite. Come on, I'll tell you what James learned from the FBI lab."

"You're not going to get your jacket?" she asked as they went back through the lobby.

Hank wore his favorite navy blue FBI National Academy Polo shirt and a pair of jeans. His weapon was holstered at his side and his badge at his belt.

"These are spring temps," he said.

LILIANA HART & LOUIS SCOTT

"Yeah, yeah," she said, chuckling as they headed across the street to the Taco and Waffle.

The restaurant was dimly lit and it took a second for her eyes to adjust. Hank pointed her toward a corner booth that looked out over Main Street. They sat silently as chips and salsa and drinks were brought.

And then the small portable police radio on his belt made a staticky sound just before Springer's voice sounded through it.

"HQ to Sheriff Davidson. You copy?"

"Go ahead HQ," Hank said.

"We need you at HQ."

"What happened?"

"Lieutenant Rodriguez arrested Bud Grant."

Lieutenant Maria Rodriguez pushed Bud Grant inside the small room and locked the thick metal door to the holding cell. She was a serious woman with dark brown skin and eyes, and she had a reputation for getting the job done. It was rare that anyone got under her skin, but Hank could tell with one glance Bud Grant had managed to do just that.

Bud was sporting a black eye and the corner of his mouth was bleeding. Hank raised a brow, and then looked at Rodriguez. She just shrugged and said, "He's got a face like a pillow."

"That's police brutality," Bud yelled through the bars. "I'm going to own this police department by the time I'm done suing you."

"Why don't you exercise your right to remain silent," Hank told him.

They left Bud pouting in his cell, and they all headed to

Hank's office so they could hear the full story. Rodriguez was the last one in the room, and she closed the door behind her, and then she stood stiff as a soldier.

Hank could tell she was waiting to see how he would react.

"Are you hurt?" Hank asked Rodriguez.

She looked surprised at first and then finally relaxed. "No, Sir."

"Good," he said. "I'm going to assume he deserved the black eye. What happened?"

"He was driving drunk," she said. "He was weaving all over the place, and even clipped a trashcan out by the curb. I followed him for a while with my dash cam before I turned on my lights. As soon as I turned them on he floored it."

"Idiot," Hank said, shaking his head.

"He's lucky he didn't kill anyone," Agatha said.

"I called in for backup, and James and Johnson blocked him at an intersection."

"That's when it got really good," James said, grinning.

"I pulled my weapon and told him to step out of the vehicle," she said. "And he was real agreeable until I went to put the cuffs on him. Then he decided it would be a good idea to kiss me."

"I'm surprised he only has one black eye," Agatha said.

"His ribs are going to be sore for a few days," Rodriguez said, a grin stretching across her face. "I was wearing my body camera."

"Good," Hank said. "That'll keep things nice and clean when his mother tries to buy him out of this. Good work."

"Thank you, sir," she replied.

"What about the vehicle?" Hank asked.

"We had it towed in," James said. "It's in inventory, so we should make the best of it and see what we can find."

"Can we do that?" Agatha asked. "Legally, I mean?"

"Sure can," James said. "Whenever we tow in a vehicle of someone we've arrested, we inventory it to make sure there's nothing missing. It's not uncommon for criminals to accuse cops of stealing their property, so as a policy, we go through and catalogue everything in the vehicle and give them a receipt for the items listed."

"Wow," Agatha said.

"You'd be surprised what people sign for," Rodriguez continued. "We've found drugs, guns and stolen property during an inventory. It's all listed on their receipt, and they'll sign off on it, thinking they'll get everything back as is. Criminals are generally dumb."

"Bud doesn't seem like an exception," Hank said. "Rodriguez, why don't you go ahead and finish booking him, and James can start the inventory."

"You got it, boss," James said, and he and Rodriguez both left the office.

"We've got to wrap him up tighter," Hank said.

"What do you mean?" Agatha asked.

"I mean everything surrounding Bud is circumstantial. We need to find a murder weapon. And we need to find witnesses who saw him in Rusty Gun or anywhere else in the area before he supposedly got to town. We've got motive because of the money angle. But we need more than that."

Agatha looked like she was going to say something and then pressed her lips together.

"What is it?" Hank asked.

"I don't buy Bud as the killer," she said.

"Me either," Hank said. "But why don't you tell me why."

"Like you said, he's an idiot. Sure he's got a temper, but he's basically a spoiled child. He's lazy, he drinks, and he has a serious lack of control. I just get the feeling that if he'd killed his father by bashing his head in, he wouldn't be able to hide it. He's not that good of a liar. You saw how bad he was earlier when we talked to him."

"Maybe he was drinking as a result of what he did," Hank said, playing devil's advocate. "So he could hide his actions behind alcohol."

"Bud Grant doesn't have an ounce of courage or fortitude. I'm not saying he's not capable of murder. Temper tantrums can lead to that kind of violence. But I think he'd be a mess afterward. I think he'd be scared. He would've left clues all over the place. Whoever killed Leland Grant wouldn't have walked out of that building without blood on him."

Hank was thoughtful for a minute, listening to Agatha's impassioned speech. He agreed with her. Bud didn't fit the profile. He was weak and whiny, and he would've been showing signs of the stress of covering up a murder if he'd really done it.

"So where does that leave us?" he asked.

"I think we need to look at someone obvious," Agatha said. "Someone unexpected at first glance. But maybe this doesn't have everything to do with Leland Grant."

"What do you mean?" Hank asked.

"What about Oddie McElroy?" Agatha asked.

Hank furrowed his brow. "What does he have to do with anything?"

"Well, when you look at everything that's been going on lately, he kind of has a lot to do with everything. Rusty Gun isn't the murder capital of the world. At least not fresh murders like this. You and I have been working cold cases

LILIANA HART & LOUIS SCOTT

from decades ago. But all of a sudden, Coil is forced to step aside as sheriff, you're barely sworn in as his temporary replacement, and then we immediately have a murder. Nothing takes confidence from voters like putting someone they don't know in power and making them feel unsafe at the same time."

Hank could see her point. And he realized he'd been too focused on how he'd been used to solving murders instead of reading between the lines of Oddie's earlier call.

"When he called," Hank said. "He told me I wasn't in the big city anymore. They do things different down here."

Agatha nodded. "It's like the wild west in a lot of ways. It can get dirty. I'm just saying I wouldn't be surprised if we opened the trunk of Bud's car and found the murder weapon and a signed confession."

CHAPTER ELEVEN

Hank hung back while the team got in and inventoried Bud's vehicle in the impound lot behind the sheriff's office. It was cold, and for once he wished he'd tossed on a jacket.

"It's not looking good, Boss," James said a few minutes later. "All we've got is a gas receipt from here in town, and another from the liquor store a county over. Both are on the day of his father's murder."

"It's not a murder weapon," Hank said. "But it proves he was in Rusty Gun and that he lied to us. It's enough for a search warrant for his parent's house."

Agatha winced.

"Yeah, I know," Hank said. "I don't want to impose on the grieving widow. But the longer we wait, the better chance they all have of coming up with alibis and destroying evidence, if Bud's past is anything to go by."

Hank saw Springer come out through the back door and head their way.

"How's it going Springer?" Hank asked.

"Making progress on the computer, but I had to rest my eyes and get some fresh air."

"Are Rodriguez and Johnson back from canvasing the area to see if anyone saw Bud Grant near his father's office?"

"She called in a few minutes ago," Springer said. "That's another reason I wanted to come out." He snugged his collar up around his neck to protect it from the wind. "She said everyone they've talked to is in a state of shock over the murder. Apparently rumors are going around that people aren't safe in their own homes, and someone is passing out pamphlets on safety precautions."

Agatha had called that one all right, Hank thought. Oddie McElroy was taking advantage of Leland Grant's murder for his own personal gain.

"Rodriguez said she heard a lot of anger against Coil, for passing the job to you instead of handling this matter himself. I'm thinking someone probably planted that seed."

"You'd be thinking right," Hank said.

"Karl said almost all of Coil's re-election signs have been taken down. It's as if he never existed."

Hank grunted and felt his anger rise. It took a lot for him to lose his temper, but if McElroy really was stooping this low then he'd just made a dangerous enemy. Hank wasn't going to stand by and watch someone do this to Coil.

"I did track down the company that does the data entry for Leland Grant," Springer said. "The warrant covers all the information, so they're going to send everything they have. But I can already tell you I have no idea what the numbers and codes mean. You're going to need a forensic accountant."

"Figures," Hank said. He hadn't even looked at a budget sheet yet to see how tight the purse strings were for extra expenses like that. "Do you have a list of his appointments yet for the day of the murder?"

"They're sending them over," he said. "Should have them before too long. Red tape. They had to send the warrant to their attorneys. They do a lot of big business and privacy is a big deal."

"We'll just have to wait and see," Hank said. "By the way, what kind of money are we talking about with regards to the monthly payments made to Bud?"

"Twenty-five hundred was deposited every Friday like clockwork,"

Hank whistled. "That's a nice chunk of change. What do you want to bet when we start digging deeper that Bud has a drug or gambling problem?"

"That's a sucker's bet," Agatha said. "Did he ever make payments to the other two kids?"

"Nothing regular," Springer said. "The occasional gift, usually coinciding with a birthday or Christmas."

Hank nodded. "As soon as those appointments come through I want you to go with Rodriguez and interview them personally."

"Me?" Springer asked surprised.

"I thought you wanted to learn?" Hank asked. "You're a sergeant. There are responsibilities that go with rank."

"I just thought maybe I'd found my niche working with computers for the department. I've enjoyed digging into the files. It's my background after all. And I like computers a lot better than people."

"Then you're in the wrong business, son," Hank said. "If you want an analyst job you need to go to a big agency. We don't have the need or budget for one full time."

Springer looked like a kid who'd just had his balloon popped. "But Sheriff, what if one of the people we interview is the killer?"

Hank took a second to breathe and remember he was

supposed to be mentoring Springer. He was young. And he'd grown up wealthy and spoiled. He barely knew what work was, and he'd done a good job during the day because he was doing something he liked to do—computers.

"Do what you're trained to do," Hank said, patiently. "Arrest them."

CHAPTER TWELVE

Lieutenant Rodriguez handed Agatha the results of a third Breathalyzer test. The first one showed Bud Grant was over the legal limit for intoxication. The last exam showed that he was now sober enough to question about his father's murder. Of course, it was time wasted and coffee invested into his sobriety, but any confession made while legally boozed up would result in a dismissal.

"Thanks, Rodriguez," Agatha said. "Let's show these to the guys. And hopefully we can get Bud questioned before the café closes. I'm starving."

"You're always starving," Rodriguez said. "I don't know where you put it all. If I ate like you I'd weigh three hundred pounds."

"Which is why I run every day," Agatha said.

Rodriguez sighed and patted her hips. "I'll just have to make do with eating salads. If you ever see me running it means someone is chasing me."

"Hank says the same thing," Agatha said.

"He's a smart man. But y'all should rethink eating at the

café. All Coil's signs are gone and they've put up signs for McElroy in the front window."

Agatha fumed. "They should know better. Coil is there almost every day. I've never seen Oddie McElroy spend much time at all in Rusty Gun. And now he's all over the place. The jerk."

Rodriguez snorted and they walked toward Hank's office, but heard voices in the break area. Hank, James and Johnson stood in a huddle, each holding a Styrofoam cup. Agatha knew Hank's cup was full of hot tea, he didn't drink coffee. Had never even tried the stuff.

"We ready to roll?" he asked, looking at the breathalyzer in Rodriguez's hand.

"Yes, Sir," she said.

"Good, you bring him into the room. I want to watch him stew for a few minutes. He's been screaming for mommy, but he hasn't asked for an attorney yet. Let's use that to our advantage."

Agatha followed Hank into the observation room, and they watched Rodriguez open the door and lead Bud inside. She put him in the chair, and he immediately got up and started pacing.

"You can't keep me here for no reason," he said.

Rodriguez didn't say anything, but turned and left the room, shutting the door behind her. They watched Bud run behind her and start pounding on the door.

"Let me out," he screamed. He pulled on the knob, but the door could only be unlocked from the outside.

They waited a good ten minutes, and Bud got more and more agitated. Going back and forth between sitting in the hardback chair and pacing around the room like a caged tiger.

"Let's go," Hank said to Agatha.

The only interrogations Agatha had ever witnessed were on TV, though she'd written plenty of them in her books. So she figured the best course of action was to let Hank handle things.

"You remember us?" Hank asked Bud.

"Sure," he said, sneering. "You woke me up. And you'll be unemployed by tomorrow. I'll never forget you."

"How touching," Hank said. "I'm a memorable kind of guy. Especially when it comes to finding killers."

Bud snorted. "Some job. My dad is dead, and you've done nothing but harass innocent, upstanding citizens."

"Is that what you are?" Hank asked. "An upstanding citizen."

"I pay your salary, don't I? Sounds pretty upstanding to me."

"From what we know about you," Hank said, "You don't pay anyone's salary. You just spend mommy and daddy's money. And then you add insult to injury and try to accost one of my cops."

"It's her word against mine," he said, shrugging. "She'll keep her mouth shut. They all do."

"You really are stupid, aren't you, Bud?" Hank asked, shaking his head in disbelief. "We've got you on camera. We've also got you cold on DWI. Even if we don't pin you for murder, you're not going to get out of here unscathed."

"Murder?" he asked, going pale. "What's this bull? I didn't murder nobody. I want to file a complaint against that lady cop. You're just trying to distract me."

"Yeah, that's what I'm doing," Hank said. "You got me."

There was a knock at the door and James stuck his head in, though Agatha knew it was planned.

"Sorry to interrupt, Sheriff," James said. "But you told

me to let you know when the judge signed the warrant. We're clear to search the Grant residence."

"What?" Bud screamed, standing up so fast his chair fell backward. "Your searching my house? *My* house?"

"I think it technically belongs to your mother, Bud," Hank said. "But since it's where you're freeloading at the moment, it's where we had to get the warrant."

"You heartless—" Bud's fists bunched and Hank put his hand on his weapon and stared him down.

"Sit down," Hank said, and Agatha watched wide-eyed as Bud thought about whether or not it was worth it to throw a punch or two.

Hank had fists like hammers, so she thought it was smart that Bud picked up his chair and sat back down. James shut the door, and she and Hank sat in the seats across from Bud. Her palms were sweaty and she casually wiped them on her jeans.

"Now Bud," Hank said. "Imagine our surprise when we find your daddy dead yesterday with his head bashed in. And then when we come out to speak to you this morning, you lie right to our faces about when you got into town. Why'd you lie?"

"I don't know what you're talking about," he said, but he was sweating and wouldn't make eye contact.

"A lie on top of a lie just makes things worse," Hank said. "Then imagine our surprise when we find out your daddy had been paying you ten grand a month and he cut you off a couple of months ago. Now we have you in the vicinity of the murder, and with motive."

"You're crazy," he said.

"How'd you kill him?"

"I—" he stopped and licked his lips. "I didn't." And then he put his face in his hands. "I don't think I did."

Agatha looked at Hank in surprise. She hadn't actually expected Bud to crack so soon.

"What do you mean you don't think you did?" Hank asked. "Did you see your father the day he died?"

"I went to see him," Bud said. "About the money. I'd tried to talk to him before, and he wouldn't listen. And I know my mom was angry with him over cutting me off. I figured she'd be able to talk him round. She always could. But he put his foot down this time. She was furious.

"So I figured I'd take another stab at it and go see him. I drove down early and then went straight in to see him. I knew if I caught him early he'd be in a better mood. He liked mornings best. We argued." He was pale now, sick looking, and he stared off with a vacant expression on his face. "We never got along. It wasn't the first fight we'd had and I didn't figure it would be the last. I stormed by him, and he reached out to stop me, but I shoved him away."

"Then what?" Hank asked.

"I ran out the back door and drove out to the liquor store of Highway 63."

"What did you hit him with?" Hank asked.

Bud looked confused. "I told you, I just shoved him and ran out. I didn't hit him with anything."

"I figured he'd call mom and give her an earful. He usually did. But he never called her."

"You've done nothing but lie to us since we first met," Agatha said. "Why should we believe you now?"

"Because now I'm telling the truth," he said, banging his fist on the table. "And I panicked when you came to see me before. I knew you'd think it was me. What would you have done in my place?"

"Tell the truth from the beginning, and not be in jail," Hank said dryly.

Bud's lips tightened, but for once he didn't have a smart-aleck remark. "Look, I'm sorry, okay."

"That's a good place to start if you're telling the truth," Hank said. "Why don't you earn some good will and tell us where the clothes you wore when you had the argument with your dad are. They need to be tested for blood."

"They're in the dirty clothes hamper in my room."

"If there's anything else you need to tell us," Hank said. "Now is the time to do it. I'm not going to be happy if I find any surprises when we search the house."

"I've told you everything," he said. "I swear."

"For your sake, I hope you're right."

CHAPTER THIRTEEN

By the time they'd gotten Bud booked on the DWI, and Rodriguez and Karl had loaded him in the back of a cruiser to transport him to the county jail, it was dark outside and his head was screaming.

Everyone was putting in overtime—which he had to be careful of now that he was in charge—so he'd cut everyone loose and sent home whoever wasn't supposed to be on swing or night shift.

He'd told Agatha he'd be home after he finished some paperwork, but he'd spent the time on the computer looking for engagement rings. He only had a slight amount of fear that she was in a different place than he was when it came to marriage. They'd never really talked about it straight out, and he knew she'd been distracted lately because of the decision to pursue a connection with the daughter she'd given up for adoption. He was with her no matter what, and he hoped these big life decisions were indicative of how she saw their future together.

He scrolled through another page of rings, reading about clarity and cut, and wanted to pull his hair out. Why did these things have to be so difficult? What was wrong with just making a decision and getting married? He'd breathe a lot easier once she said, "I do."

The bell above the front door sounded, and he knew there wasn't anyone out there to greet the visitor, so he closed his laptop and checked the surveillance cameras to see who it was.

An older man in a heavy coat stood looking around the area as if he were going to start measuring for curtains and furniture, so Hank decided to see if he could be of any help and used the intercom to speak to him.

"Can I help you?" Hank asked.

"Is the sheriff in? I need to see him."

Hank thought about that for a second and reminded himself this was a small county. People expected to have access to officials. But years of training didn't disappear and he placed his pistol on his lap, keeping a hand on it just in case.

"Come on back," Hank said, and hit the buzzer that unlocked the door between the reception area and the squad room.

He listened to footsteps coming down the hall, and then the man was standing in his doorway. He was a good-sized man, probably in his mid-seventies, and he reminded Hank of a tough old boot.

"Can I help you?" Hank asked.

"I'm thinking you must be beyond help," the man said.

Hank stayed silent and raised a brow. He wasn't worried about a threat—he could handle an old man—but he also wasn't going to take any disrespect in his own office.

"You must be out of your danged mind pulling the stunt you did tonight. You'll be sorry about that. Mark my words."

"If you mean taking a drunk driver and murder suspect

off the streets," Hank said slowly, "Then, no. I'm not sorry at all. You're welcome."

"I don't care for smart mouths."

"I'd ask who you are, but I recognize your voice from your call earlier today. Though it sounds like you've sobered up some. Hello, Oddie."

"Don't get too comfortable behind that desk, boy. It's going to be mine before too long."

"For the time being, it's mine," Hank said. "So watch your step. I'm just about to head out for the day, and you are too."

"You're not going to push me around," McElroy said. "I'm a tax-paying citizen."

"I'm really getting tired of hearing that from people who think it means something," Hank said. He slipped his weapon back in the holster and then stood up, gathering his stuff.

"Let me give you a piece of advice," McElroy said, taking a step back when Hank used his body to move him back into the hallway. He closed his office door and locked it.

"I'll pass," Hank said, walking back toward the front and Oddie scrambled to keep up behind him. He wanted to be in full view of the cameras.

"If you know what's good for you, you'll call that señorita and tell her to high-tail that boy back to his mama's house. Everybody knows he didn't kill his daddy."

"And I suppose you know who did?" Hank asked.

"I know lots of things," McElroy said, not breaking his gaze from Hank's. And in the depth of his eyes Hank saw that a man like Oddie McElroy could kill with no remorse. "And one thing I do know is you're barking up the wrong tree with that boy. Leland Grant had a terrible accident.

That's all it was. Time to put this away and focus on other things."

"I appreciate your stalwart investigation skills," Hank said. "But I think I'll keep bumbling along to find the real killer. Who knows? Maybe he's right under my nose."

McElroy's eyes narrowed, and Hank felt like he was in an old west showdown, waiting for the other man to draw.

"Maybe he is," McElroy said. "And maybe you ought to be careful where you stick that nose of yours. You're an outsider here. Don't have a lot of friends to back you up."

"I've got plenty of friends, and all of them are in just the right places," Hank said, reading between the lines. He wanted to get home to Agatha. They were going to have to be careful, and watch over their shoulders until the killer was caught.

"Everything all right out here?" Springer asked, coming out from his office.

"Never better," Hank said. "I was just about to walk Mr. McElroy out."

"You're Doris Springer's boy, ain't ya?" McElroy asked.

"Yessir," Springer said.

"Known your mama a long time. Good Christian woman. I was just telling Mr. Davidson here that it's a shame about Leland Grant's death. Terrible accident. But these things happen when you get old and feeble. He just fell and bumped his head. It's a terrible tragedy. I'm sure you agree."

"It's a tragedy all right," Springer said.

"I knew you were a sharp kid," McElroy said. "You're probably looking at a promotion after I win the election. I want loyal men in high positions."

Springer's brows rose almost to his hairline, and Hank knew this was a defining moment for Springer because it would speak to his character and the kind of cop he'd be in the future. He hoped he wasn't disappointed, but he'd learned not to get his hopes up.

"I meant it's a tragedy about Mr. Grant's murder," Springer said. "The coroner said plain as day that he was bashed in the head with something. He couldn't have done it himself. But we'll figure out who did it soon enough. We've got leads."

"You're making a mistake," McElroy said. "Your mama would be disappointed."

"Don't worry about my mama," Springer said. "She's from the south. She can chew you up, spit you out, and serve a coffeecake with a smile all at the same time."

"Well then," Hank said, pleased. "I guess we'll keep following the evidence and facts instead of your say so. But we appreciate you stopping by."

"You boys have just made the biggest mistake of your lives. You could've had the world on a platter if you'd only done what I told you to. No one crosses Oddie McElroy. No one."

"That sounds like a threat," Hank said softly.

McElroy didn't bat an eyelash as he stared him down. The man was power hungry and used to getting his own way.

Springer cleared his throat and said, "Why don't I escort Mr. McElroy out before he gets himself arrested."

"Thanks for the offer, Springer, but it's my night to take out the trash." Hank knew he was goading the man, but he didn't care.

"What did you say?" McElroy moved so he was chest to chest with Hank, but Hank didn't back down. He could defend himself if it came to that, but Hank knew the cameras were rolling and wanted to get as much of Oddie's visit on tape as possible.

"I said it's time for you to leave. I don't care about your threats or if you think you're going to be sheriff. The fact is that I'm the sheriff, and you've worn out your welcome. And if you say one more dumb thing, I'm going to toss you in a cell for the night. I don't care who you know or who you think your friends are. You're just a sad old man who wants to impress his friends by wearing a badge and misusing your power. You're nothing now, and you'll be nothing then, because a badge won't make you what you're not—a man."

McElroy's fury was palpable, and Hank knew he'd just made a powerful enemy. But McElroy turned on his heel and slammed out of the sheriff's office.

CHAPTER FOURTEEN

Friday

"Hank, you going to sleep the day away?" Agatha asked, knocking on the door.

He'd worked late the night before, and she'd noticed he seemed to be worried about something, but he hadn't told her what it was. Though it hadn't gone past her notice that he made sure the doors and windows were all locked tight, and he had weapons strategically placed around the house.

She'd already been out on her morning run since the weather was nice again, but she'd only done three miles instead of ten. She'd noticed a black Lincoln sedan several times as she'd rounded corners, and it had made her uneasy so she'd run back to the house as fast as she could. But Hank was still asleep when she got there.

He rarely slept past seven o'clock, but it was almost a quarter after. Their relationship had reached a crossroads when she'd moved in. She knew the town was talking, but she didn't care. Her business was her own. At least, that's what she told herself.

But this new dynamic was weird. They weren't

married. But they were a couple who, in her mind, was moving in that direction. But they acted like roommates instead of what they'd had before when they were living separately. She didn't know if Hank was trying to be careful to not cross the boundary line or what, but she was going crazy. It was time to move things to the next level, because living on opposite sides of the house in separate bedrooms was a short-term solution. She wanted a ring, a wedding, and a shared bedroom. And she wanted to get rid of the hideous wallpaper in the dining room, but she figured first things first.

She showered and dressed for the day in jeans and another Henley, and layered a seasonal vest over it in navy. The vest hid her weapon well. She'd been used to carrying a weapon in her purse, but wearing it on her body had taken some getting used to now that she was an official detective.

There wasn't a peep coming from Hank's room, so Agatha grabbed her keys and decided to head on into the office. She didn't want to miss serving the warrant on the Grant residence. She'd just put her hand on the knob when she heard Hank's door open.

"You leaving?" he asked.

"Yeah, sleepyhead. It's almost eight o'clock."

"Don't leave without me," he said. "We might have a problem."

With that, he shut the door and left her standing with her mouth open. "Well, then. I guess I'll just sit around and wait."

She could've done some research for her latest book, or answered business emails, but she wasn't really in the mood. Her fingers tapped impatiently on the arm of the chair, and she did a couple of Sudoku puzzles on her phone before she heard the door open again.

"Finally," she said. "What the heck is going on? I don't want to miss them serving that warrant."

"I had a visitor at the office," Hank said. "Oddie McElroy decided to pay me a visit, and it wasn't pleasant. We need to be extra careful. He's a dangerous man. And I think you're right. He knows exactly who killed Leland Grant—either him or someone he knows that he'll cover for. But we need to find a connection between Grant and McElroy."

She told him about the car she saw following her on her morning run, and was glad she listened to her intuition to come home early.

"Are you going to come with us to serve the warrant?" she asked.

"No, I'm going to start making inquiries on Oddie McElroy. Springer said that Leland Grant served on the state finance committee. If we take what we know about Grant, which is that he was a good ethical guy, then maybe he found something that didn't look right."

"Makes sense," she said, leaning over to give him a kiss. "Be careful."

"You too," he said.

"I'll call you if we find anything at the Grant's."

"Do me a favor," Hank asked as they walked to the front door. "Drop Oddie McElroy's name to Mrs. Grant and watch carefully to see how she reacts. I'm playing a hunch."

Agatha sat in the back seat behind Karl and James in their cruiser to the Grant residence. They had their lights on, but no sirens, and she knew everyone would be watching.

Everything had to be by the book from here on out. No mess ups.

"You drive like an old lady," James said to Karl. "By the time we get out there everyone in Rusty Gun will know we're serving a warrant."

"I think we're being followed," Karl said, slowing down even more.

There was a new model pickup truck with all the bells and whistles about two hundred yards behind them, but it was hard to see the license plate.

"Keep going to the Grant's," James said. "We're sitting ducks out here if there's a threat. We'll see if he keeps following us."

Karl pressed the accelerator and so did the truck. Whoever was driving didn't even pretend to hide what they were doing.

"Let's see if he's dumb enough to follow us onto private property," James said. "Then we can have a little conversation, and get an I.D."

Sure enough, as soon as they pulled through the open gates and headed down the long private drive, the truck turned in behind them.

"Let's go shake things up a little," James said. "I've got my body cam, and Karl can call in for backup if we need it."

Agatha nodded and got out of the car, making sure her badge and weapon were visible. Her heart raced as she and James approached the driver's side door, and the window rolled down before James could knock on it.

"ID and registration," James said.

"You don't know who I am, boy?"

"I know you're making a nuisance of yourself, and hindering a murder investigation. You're following a marked police vehicle at a close pace, which can be seen as suspicious activity or a threat. So I don't really care who you are."

"I'm going to be your boss come election day," he said. "And we just happened to be going to the same place. Just a coincidence."

"This is your residence?" James asked.

"No, but Evelyn is a close personal friend, and I'll be here in her time of need if you're going to harass her."

"You're trespassing on private property, and interfering with duly sworn officers from doing their job. Everyone is about to be vacated from the premises while we execute our warrant. So I suggest you turn around and head back to where you came from before you get in trouble."

"Evelyn needs me," he insisted. "She's a wreck. You've already put her boy in jail. What more are you going to put her through?"

"Funny you didn't mention her husband," Agatha said. "He's the victim. The one who was murdered? We're trying to catch his killer."

"Husband?" Oddie said, going red in the face. "He wasn't much of a husband. Or a father. He was an old fool who didn't know what he was doing half the time. Age was catching up with him, and it showed. Made mistakes left and right. His business wouldn't have lasted the year."

"You sure know a lot about Mr. Grant's personal life," James said.

"I told you I'm close to the family," he insisted. "And Evelyn wants me here."

"Evelyn seemed to love her husband very much," Agatha said. "She was devastated when we delivered the news about his death. She said she felt guilty for not spending enough time with him. Always heading off to Austin."

His face got even redder, and she knew he couldn't dispute anything she said without giving away more about his and Evelyn's relationship. He pressed his lips together, gave them both a look that could kill, then slammed his truck in reverse and sped out of the driveway.

"Hank's hunch pays off," Agatha said.

"They usually do," agreed James.

CHAPTER FIFTEEN

Hank and Springer started digging into Oddie McElroy and any relationship he might have had with Leland Grant the minute he walked in the office. He called in favors at the FBI and Texas Rangers, and hopefully someone could find some information.

Hank's gut was never wrong, and Oddie McElroy had it screaming.

Agatha called around lunch. Nothing had come up with the search warrant, and they'd found nothing resembling a murder weapon. And Bud's clothes didn't have a speck of anything that looked like blood on them.

But she'd also filled him in on the conversation she'd had with Oddie that morning, and how he'd reacted when she'd spoken about Evelyn Grant. And apparently, Evelyn wasn't quite as good at hiding her feelings, because Agatha said she all but confessed to their affair when she brought up Oddie's name.

Hank had a feeling that there'd been someone else in Evelyn Grant's life. And there was something about the way Oddie had insisted that Bud was innocent and a certain look in his eye that made Hank think the connection between Oddie and the Grant family might run deep. But Oddie hadn't cared at all about finding Leland's killer. Which meant he cared about someone else in the family on a level that would make him act like an insane person. And in his experience, the only person who could make a man insane was a woman.

"Woohoo!" he heard Springer call from the other room.

Hank hopped up from his desk and ran to Springer's office.

"What is it?" Hank asked excitedly.

"I just got Grant's appointments for the day of his murder. And Guess who was scheduled to meet him around the time he was killed?"

"Oddie McElroy," Hank said, seeing the name on the list. "The guy must be an idiot to think he can keep buying his way out of anything he wants, or by using his connections. Connections only get you so far, especially if your ship is sinking."

"We can put him in the vicinity at TOD, but what's the motive?" Springer asked. "There's got to be a reason."

"I believe Evelyn Grant and Oddie were having an affair," Hank said.

Springer raised his brows. "Let me call my mom and ask her. She'd know if something like that was going on. No one can keep a secret like that in a town this size."

"That's a good idea," Hank said.

"I want you to dig deeper now that you've got access to all the clients. People don't generally make appointments to murder someone. But if McElroy was a client, maybe he and Grant had a disagreement over taxes or investments."

"I'm on it, boss," Springer said.

Hank went back to his desk and glanced at the newspaper his secretary had placed there early that morning. The *Rusty Gun Gazette* didn't have much to offer in the way of news, but on the front page was a picture of Oddie McElroy on the golf course in the middle of a swing. It was an ad for his fundraiser at the country club. It was an open invitation for the whole community to come out and meet the future sheriff of Bell County.

Hank was thinking it might not be a bad idea to take him up on the invitation. In fact, maybe he needed to turn the tide on old Oddie. Maybe Hank needed to show up like a bad penny every time Oddie turned a corner. Get under his skin. If he killed Leland Grant, and there was definitely a possibility he did, then Grant had the kind of temper that would make him stupid.

Hank tossed the paper into the trash, and leaned back in his chair.

"What's up?" Agatha asked, coming into the office and taking a seat on the corner of his desk.

"I'm just plotting," he said.

"Hopefully about Oddie McElroy," she said. "Springer told me to tell you as I passed by that he called his mother. Apparently you and I are the only two people in Rusty Gun who didn't know Evelyn Grant and Oddie were having an affair. Evidently, it's been going on for years. Springer said the Grants' marriage was for show more than anything. Leland was married to his work and money, and he didn't particularly care what Evelyn did. So she did what she wanted."

"Huh," Hank said. "Then the affair wouldn't necessarily be a motive for killing the competition."

"Doesn't look like it," Agatha said. "Which means we need to pin him down somewhere else."

"How do you feel about golf?" Hank asked her.

"I like it in theory," she said. "I have a terrible short game, and I can make it about nine holes before I start to get bored and want snacks. Why?"

"I was thinking we should go to a fundraiser tomorrow. Play a few holes."

"You want to get under his skin," Agatha said, thoughtfully. "I like it."

"Thank you," he said.

James knocked on the door. "We got something."

"Come on in," Hank said, coming to his feet.

Springer and James came in and James said, "I got a reply from the FBI crime lab. You must have called in some crazy favors, because I wasn't expecting these results for a couple of weeks. Anyway, they were able to determine the specimens removed from Grant's wound by the coroner, and also the metallic flakes we got from the office chair."

"Anything familiar?" Hank asked.

"It looks like the materials collected were wood, graphite fiber-reinforced epoxy, and a zirconia ceramic. So no, I have no idea what that is."

"I thought it was just metallic flakes? Like a pipe or something," Agatha said.

"No, according to this report it looks like there were multiple items that transferred material as a result of the blow to Mr. Grant's skull."

"How about the stuff from the chair?" Hank asked.

James ran a finger across the pages looking for the exact spot of reference.

"Here we go. Looks like boron fiber-reinforced epoxy and titanium."

"Well, I'm no scientist, but that doesn't sound like a pipe," Hank said. "Can you reach back out to the crime lab and ask for a list of common objects that would have those material combinations?"

"Sure thing," James agreed.

"What about you Springer?" Hank asked, feeling a lot warmer toward the kid after their run-in with McElroy the night before.

"I'm not finding any files labeled McElroy, and I can't find that they've had professional meetings in the past. At least not at Grant's office."

Hank thought for a few minutes. "Let's look at the players closest to Leland Grant. His wife. She's moving up my list as a suspect. I don't think she committed the murder. Her alibi checks out. But the affair with Oddie could've escalated. Maybe they wanted something more permanent. And she stands to inherit a lot of money and property so far as we know without seeing a will.

"We've got Bud. He's an idiot, but I don't think he's a killer. But he confessed to being there around the time Grant was killed. He admitted to shoving his father, and leaving him there, without checking to see if he was hurt. Oddie's appointment would have been about that time. Maybe he didn't know Grant used the outside company to keep his calendar straight. Maybe it was all informal. Oddie gives Grant a call and says, "Hey, do you mind if I swing by so we can chat for a few minutes," and unbeknownst to Oddie, Leland has it committed to the calendar so there are no interruptions."

"And then Oddie walks in just after Bud runs out, finds Grant on the floor, and finishes the job," Agatha said. "It makes it easy to push the blame onto Bud."

"You said something when we first started digging, Springer," Hank said. "Something I kept thinking about."

"What's that, Sheriff?" Springer asked.

"You said Grant was on the state finance committee. And I took the liberty to look up what that job entails. Grant was in charge of overseeing the finance laws for any elected or appointed officials. But also any candidates. He makes sure campaign funds are being used correctly and in accordance with the law."

"Oh," they all said at once.

"We need a warrant to get a copy of the campaign finance report Oddie submitted to the state. And we need a warrant for the state records Mr. Grant kept. He wouldn't have those in his business computer. Let's get this locked down today."

"We still need the murder weapon to tie a bow on it," Agatha said.

CHAPTER SIXTEEN

Saturday

Once they found the right places to look, all the pieces started falling into place. No amount of money or influence in the world was going to save Oddie McElroy this time.

It was another sunny, yet chilly day in the forties, but it was supposed to warm up in the afternoon. It was a great day for golf, and a great day for an arrest.

Agatha wore cargo pants and a long-sleeved polo in navy with a pair of bright white golf shoes, and her mouth twitched when she saw Hank was dressed almost exactly the same as she was.

They arrived at the sheriff's office, and Springer, James, Rodriguez, and Karl Johnson were already there waiting. They'd gotten the information they needed from the state and the FBI lab late the night before, and they were all excited to get the case wrapped up and take Oddie McElroy down.

They had a quick briefing, and Hank gave everyone their assignments. Finding the murder weapon was key, and they had warrants to deliver to Oddie. He wasn't going to be happy.

He'd called for other deputies to meet them all at the country club for crowd control, and to detain anyone who tried to get away. Hank let Rodriguez take the lead, lights and sirens blaring, and then fell in line with the rest of the gang. This had truly been a team effort, and they all wanted to see it through to the end.

They met the other deputies just before they turned into the country club, and they sped into the parking lot among all the high-priced cars and golf carts. There were a couple of early teams already on the course, but there was a large crowd in the lobby along with television cameras.

A man in a suit was the first to see the police cars and ran out to intervene before a scene could be made.

"Can I help you, officer?" the man asked. "I'm Charles Wilson. I'm the manager here at the club."

"It's sheriff, actually," Hank said. "Sheriff Davidson. And we have a couple of warrants to serve." He handed the paper to Wilson. "We're here to search the grounds, the club house, locker rooms. We believe one of your members killed Leland Grant."

"Mr. Grant was also a member," Wilson said, looking shell-shocked. "He was a very nice man. It was terrible to hear of his passing. Whatever you need, me or my staff are happy to help."

"Thank you," Hank said, directing his deputies to fan out.

"What in Sam Hill is going on?" Oddie asked, pushing his way through the cameras and crowds to confront Hank.

Hank was ready for him. "This is a warrant to search that truck of yours and your locker here at the club, including your golf bag."

Oddie took the warrant and tore it in half, tossing it on the ground. "Your warrants don't mean anything here. This is my territory."

"Yeah, your understanding of the law is pretty terrible for someone who wants to be sheriff," Hank said. "I've been on the phone with the state ethics committee about your campaign spending. It seems Leland Grant shared his findings with several people, including the FBI. It was only a matter of time before they came for you. Did you really think killing Grant would be the end of your troubles?"

Oddie paled. "I don't know what you're talking about."

"Sure you do," Hank said, smiling. It wasn't his nice smile and Oddie took a step back. "We've got charges of money laundering, bribery, misuse of funds. Enough to send you to prison for the rest of your life. Now you add murder to that and you're looking at the death penalty." Hank shook his head. "You're so proud of the people you know in high places who will do anything for you because you're lining their pockets, except at the end of the day, not one of those people were willing to go down with you to save you. You need better friends, McElroy."

"I didn't kill Leland," Oddie insisted. "You can't prove anything. You're just grasping at straws. Isn't Bud sitting in jail because *he's* your prime suspect?"

"Sheriff," Rodriguez called out, holding up a golf bag. "His driver is missing, but the cover is here. It lit up like a Christmas tree when hit with luminal."

"Where'd you dump the driver?" Hank asked Oddie. "We got the report back from the FBI lab. Your golf clubs were specially made, weren't they? You had them coated with a gold primer. Very unusual. And a terrible idea for a murder weapon. That gold ended up in Leland Grant's head when you hit him."

"Got it, Sheriff," James called out. "It was in his truck. He wiped it down, but he couldn't remove all traces."

"Nice job," Hank said. "We've got you cold."

"No," he said, shaking his head, looking shell-shocked. He caught a glimpse of the cameras, all pointed in his direction, and the crowd of people who looked just as shocked as he was. He was finished.

"Tell me," Agatha said. "Did Evelyn Grant know you were going to kill her husband that morning? Did the two of you hatch this plan together so you could have a life together?"

"Evelyn had nothing to do with any of this," Oddie said angrily, taking a step toward Agatha. "Nothing. Leave her alone!"

With one swipe of his forearm, Oddie struck out at Agatha, but Hank moved quickly, stepping between them before he could make contact. Hank blocked the punch and delivered one of his own to Oddie's midsection, and then spun him so he faced the wall, jerking his arm behind his back while Oddie was still trying to catch his breath.

"Springer," Hank called out. "Let's get him cuffed."

Springer looked like a kid on Christmas morning. "You got it, Sheriff." He snapped on the cuffs, and then his grin spread when he heard his mother telling one of the cameramen that it was her son arresting Oddie McElroy, and how proud she was of him.

The reporters were all talking over each other, trying to get to Hank, but he put his hands up to quiet them.

"This is just part of the job. And it probably would've been done a lot faster if Sheriff Reggie Coil had been behind the helm instead of me. But that was part of Oddie's plan. You've got a great sheriff and this is a great and safe community. It's time to bring Coil back and get the real criminals like McElroy out of positions they abuse."

Hank led Agatha to the car, but he was smiling. The crowd had started yelling Coil for Sheriff. It was a good day.

EPILOGUE

"I, Reginald Walker Coil, do solemnly swear, that I will faithfully execute the duties of the office of Sheriff for Bell County, of the State of Texas, and will to the best of my ability preserve, protect, and defend the Constitution and laws of the United States and of this State, so help me God."

"Congratulations, Sheriff Coil on your re-election and return to the Office of the Sheriff," said Judge Thomas Trammel.

"Thank you, Sir."

Hank held Agatha's hand as he watched his best friend being sworn-in for a new four-year term as sheriff. Coil's wife and son clung to him while reporters and members of his staff circled around to commemorate the occasion.

"Hey, Boss," Springer said.

"It's just Hank now," he said.

"Right," he said. "I just wanted to thank you. You really helped me a lot. I won't forget it."

"Springer, you're going to be a good cop. I'm proud of you."

Springer looked like he was going to cry, so he hurried

off to stand with the rest of the deputies that had come to the swearing-in.

All the charges against Coil had been dropped. He'd been viciously and falsely attacked for having given his entire life to protect the very same people who cast false allegations against him. In the end, most of those same accusers who sat on the state's law enforcement ethics board were removed and charged with criminal conspiracy once Oddie McElroy started to spill the beans in hopes of a plea deal.

As the small county court room cleared, Coil hurried over to them. He embraced Hank and held tight. He couldn't say the words he was feeling, and Hank understood that. They'd been through a lot together over the years, and they'd always had each other's backs. And they always would.

"Thank you," Coil finally said. "I owe you."

"You owe me nothing," Hank said. "I have something for you." Hank held out his hand and in it was the gold sheriff's badge.

Coil let out a shaky breath and took it. It was a badge that weighed heavy, no matter who held it. "I'm going to take the family down to the Kettle Café to celebrate. Want to join us?"

"No way," Agatha said, frowning. "They ditched you in support of McElroy. They took down your signs"

"Actually," Hank said. "McElroy owned the lease on the building and threatened to evict them unless they showed their support."

"Seriously?"

"Yep," Coil agreed. "The manager called me to apologize and let me know they had no choice."

"We'll pass on lunch, but thanks. You and your family

enjoy the time together." Hank slapped him on the shoulder. "Just think, you'll be back behind that desk, dealing with all the politics bright and early in the morning. I missed retirement."

Coil grinned and pulled Hank close so only he could hear what he had to say. "Don't get too comfortable. You've only got two weeks to figure out how to propose to Agatha."

SNEAK PEEK: BLAZING SADDLES

On Sale Now

Tuesday, February 14th

Today was the day Hank Davidson's life would change forever.

He'd thought about it, worried about it, talked about it, considered it, and reconsidered it. And finally, he'd made the decision to propose to Agatha Harley. And he was almost sure he could do it without making a fool of himself.

It had been almost three years since he'd moved to Rusty Gun, Texas. He'd spent his career as an FBI-trained serial killer hunter, but his heart had no longer been in it, and he'd turned in his gun and badge for the lazy days of retirement.

It had been Sheriff Reggie Coil, his long-time friend, who'd first invited Hank to Rusty Gun so he could disappear and get some much-needed R&R. But never in a million years had the big city murder cop ever thought he'd become a permanent citizen of the sleepy, southern town. Much less fall in love there.

Agatha was his perfect match. She'd once had dreams of solving high-profile criminal cases as a forensic anthropologist, but a stalker had changed the course of her life and sent her back to Rusty Gun. She'd persevered through more than he could imagine and still managed to become a successful author, writing about the very crimes she first dreamt of solving.

Agatha enjoyed small town living and was content to spend her days reading, researching and writing about the career she no longer pursued. But Hank had changed all of that when the two clashed while investigating their first cold case together.

Their relationship was what some might call a slow simmer, but Hank was methodical in every aspect of his life. It's what made him one of the best homicide detectives in the world. It was what also caused him to wait months to propose while he planned everything down to the minutest detail.

Though to say he planned it without help would be a lie. Preparations for solving a crime were a lot different than preparations for romance. And he wasn't afraid to admit his skills in romance were...lacking. He didn't understand why people couldn't just make a decision to get married and do it, but in his experience, women tended to disapprove of the cut and dried technique. And more importantly, he wanted to make it special for Agatha.

And for that, he'd had to get Agatha's best friend, Heather Cartwright, involved. He and Heather had never seen eye to eye on anything, and she was one of Hank's least favorite people on the planet, but they both loved Agatha and had her best interests at heart.

Heather's favorite pastime was marriage and divorce, so she knew a thing or two about romantic proposals.

She'd also accumulated a lot of wealth during her marriages, so she knew all the best places stay and eat. Which is why Hank had booked adjoining suites at a luxury hotel on the Riverwalk in San Antonio, a private driver, and reservations for a seven-course dinner for Valentine's Day, where he'd eventually get down on one knee and pop the question. Just the thought had him breaking out in a sweat.

Hank patted the ring box in his pocket that he'd been carrying around for several days. He was afraid to let it out of his sight. He'd driven to Austin and picked it out himself, finding an unique design that reminded him of Agatha— because she was definitely unique in every way.

He knew his mind should be on the upcoming weekend getaway, but he couldn't help but be distracted by the email he'd gotten from the FBI field office in Philadelphia—his old stomping ground. He needed to get his emotions under control before he saw Agatha. She was very intuitive, especially where he was concerned, and she'd know something was wrong.

It was the only news that could have elicited this kind of response. It was his past come back to haunt him. The only case he'd worked that had ever gone unsolved. The Cooper Cove Boys had robbed banks all over the east coast. They were brilliant in their execution. Like a military operation. And then they upped the stakes and added murder to their list of crimes.

Hank wasn't proud to say that politics and red tape had gotten in the way of bringing justice to the victims. The FBI wanted to make sure the headlines focused on the robberies and not the murders. It brought better press and looked sexier in print. And the FBI outplayed their hand, setting up a sting that never came to fruition because the Copper

Cove Boys got wind of it, took the fortune they'd amassed, and went underground.

"And now they're back," Hank whispered. And the FBI wanted him to help with the investigation.

Even a year or so ago, he would have jumped at the chance to get back on board. His pride was at stake. It was the one case that got away from him. But his priorities had changed. There were other investigators who could lead the charge and bring the ruthless gang down. But not him. He was looking to the future. It was time to get engaged and start his life with Agatha.

He'd been amazed how easily everyone had been able to deceive Agatha into taking the trip to San Antonio for the weekend. Coil's recent suspension and reinstatement as sheriff had played into the scenario perfectly. Agatha hadn't thought a thing of it when Coil said he'd book the trip as a thank you to them both for stepping up to the plate and taking over while he'd been out, and also for exposing all the corruption that had been going on during the election.

But Agatha had been thrilled for the chance to get away, and hadn't asked too many questions.

"This is exciting," she said, looking out the window as their plane landed. "We're both in need of a break and this is going to be perfect. I'm going to eat my way through pounds of chips and salsa."

Hank chuckled. The gleam in her eyes was like that of a kid in a candy store. "And when you get too full, I'll roll you back to the hotel so you can fall into a carb coma."

"That's one of the many reasons I love you," she said, squeezing his hand.

Hank let out a breath when he saw the driver waiting for them at the airport. Everything was going to plan. He owed Heather big time. Check-in went smoothly, and the concierge gave him a thumb's up out of Agatha's view. Hank hoped that meant the champagne and chocolate covered strawberries were waiting in the room.

Hank had lived life on a policeman's budget, so he'd never stayed in a hotel like this one before. It was built like a fort, complete with stone battlements and cannons in the parapets. The décor was lush and expensive and old, and he saw from the placard on the wall that it had, in fact, been a real fort during the Mexican-American War.

The man who'd checked them in was guiding them to their suite in the top tower. The suite had two bedrooms and two baths, but was connected by a common living area. The temptation had been enormous, but they'd both been careful to keep separate living quarters, at home and when they traveled. He *really* hoped they had a short engagement.

"Wow," Agatha said, when their guide opened their door and let them in. "Gorgeous."

Hank barely noticed the open space or the balcony that looked out over the Riverwalk. The champagne and strawberries were laid out next to a bouquet of flowers, just as planned, but his throat was closing up and he started to feel the panic of what was to come.

"You okay?" she asked, putting a hand on his arm.

"Yeah, I'm just warm," he said, and tipped the hotel employee before shutting the door behind him.

"Is that a hot tub in the corner?" Agatha asked.

Hank chuckled uncomfortably, but it came out more as a croak.

"Everything is beautiful," she said, smelling the bouquet of yellow roses.

"Happy Valentine's Day," he said, his voice hoarse.

The smile that spread across her face was worth every worry and hours of time spent planning for the weekend.

"I love it," she said, her eyes glistening with tears.

It was then he realized how little time he spent trying to romance Agatha. He took her no-nonsense attitude and drive to get the job done for granted. She still had these hidden soft spots, and it was important for him to remember that.

She threw herself into his arms and kissed him, surprising him with her enthusiasm. By the time she let go, they were both out of breath.

"Wow," she said again, blushing this time. "This really is special. I'm so glad you attacked me on your lawn the first day we met."

He barked out a laugh in surprise. "You tripped over the sprinkler."

"Yes, after you blasted me with a garden hose."

"You were trespassing."

"There's no such thing in a small town," she said. "I was just being neighborly."

"Nosy," he corrected. "Champagne?"

"Of course," she said.

He poured her a glass and made her a plate with the strawberries. "We have dinner reservations in a couple of hours. I suggest you take these, put some bubbles in the tub, and soak until you're puny. I'll meet you back out here at eighteen-thirty."

Hank tried to nap, but he was too wired up, so he turned on the TV. When that didn't hold his attention he went ahead and showered and dressed in his dark gray suit and a pale purple shirt and tie the woman at the store helped him pick out.

He'd left his champagne untouched, wanting a clear head, and he was pacing back and forth in their common area when he heard her door open. He turned to face her and the spit dried up in his mouth and his lungs stopped working.

She wore a dress the color of crushed strawberries, and it skimmed her long, lean body in a way that made him want to keep her all to himself and not let any other man set eyes on her. The strappy black shoes had her standing slightly taller than him, but he didn't mind. Agatha was simply a natural beauty, with eyes that changed between blue and green, dark lashes, and dark hair she'd been letting grow and let hang in loose curls around her shoulders. Hank loved that she was comfortable in who she was, and her confidence drew every eye to her when she was in a crowd.

"Wow," Hank stumbled over what to say.

Her smile lit the room. "Thanks," she said. "I'm ready when you are."

Their driver took them to the historic district to what looked like a renovated old his. It was simple and elegant, and there were several well-dressed couples being let out at the front doors for the special Valentine's dinner.

Despite the number of couples, the tables weren't crammed in so they were all sitting on top of each other, and they were led to a corner table near the fireplace that was secluded and romantic.

"I'm impressed," Agatha said. "You've pulled out all the stops."

Hank just smiled, reminding himself to thank Heather again. He was even able to sit with his back to the wall so he could observe the entire room. Police habits never died.

Wine would be served with each course, and they got lost in conversation like they normally did. But the proposal was all he could think about. When should he do it? After the appetizer? During dessert?"

He didn't think he could wait, so he slipped his hand

into his coat pocket and grabbed the ring box. He shifted his weight to slide from the chair smoothly onto one knee, and he sucked in a deep breath just before the restaurant erupted in applause.

Across the room was another man who'd just stolen Hank's thunder and proposed to the shocked woman sitting across from him. Hank tightened his fist in frustration and let go of the ring box so it stayed in his pocket. He'd wait until the next course.

He'd felt more relaxed after the appetizer and first wine course, so he cleared his throat and decided to try again. He reached for the box just as the restaurant erupted in applause yet again. He growled aloud this time, causing Agatha to look at him with concern.

It happened again after the salad course. And again after the main course. Dessert was going to be his turn, come hell or high water, and he looked around the restaurant ferociously daring anyone to contradict him.

"Agatha," Hank said, stopping their conversation abruptly.

He grasped the ring box and scooted his chair back so it scraped across the wooden floor. And he moved to get down on one knee just as there was a collective gasp through the restaurant. He scanned the restaurant, looking for his nemesis, and his gaze locked on his target. The man and his new fiancé looked like they'd already had too much to drink.

"Hank, are you all right?" Agatha asked, her attention caught between him and the happy couple.

He was so focused on his plans being interrupted that it barely registered when his enemy shook the champagne bottle before he tried to open it. Hank saw the sommelier rush toward the man, trying to head him off before he drenched everyone around him in champagne. But it was too late.

Hank heard the resounding *pop* of the cork that seemed more like a gunshot in the closed-in space, and then he felt nothing but pain as the cork found its target right in the center of his forehead. He slid from his chair, the world spinning, and then there was nothing but black.

Liliana and I have loved sharing these stories in our Harley & Davidson Mystery Series with you.

There are many more adventures to be had for Aggie and Hank. Make sure you stay up to date with life in Rusty Gun, Texas by signing up for our emails.

Thanks again and please be sure to leave a review where you bought each story and, recommend the series to your friends.

Kindly,
Scott & Liliana

Enjoy this book? You can make a big difference

Reviews are so important in helping us get the word out about Harley and Davidson Mystery Series. If you've enjoyed this adventure Liliana & I would be so grateful if you would take a few minutes to leave a review (it can be as short as you like) on the book's buy page.

Thanks,
Scott & Liliana

Down and Dirty

Dirty Deeds

Dirty Laundry

Dirty Money

A Dirty Job

Addison Holmes Mystery Series

Whiskey Rebellion

Whiskey Sour

Whiskey For Breakfast

Whiskey, You're The Devil

Whiskey on the Rocks

Whiskey Tango Foxtrot

Whiskey and Gunpowder

Books by Liliana Hart and Scott Silverii

The Harley and Davidson Mystery Series

The Farmer's Slaughter

A Tisket a Casket

I Saw Mommy Killing Santa Claus

Get Your Murder Running

Deceased and Desist

Malice In Wonderland

Tequila Mockingbird

Gone With the Sin

The Gravediggers

The Darkest Corner

Gone to Dust

Say No More

Lawmen of Surrender (MacKenzies-1001 Dark Nights)

1001 Dark Nights: Captured in Surrender

1001 Dark Nights: The Promise of Surrender

Sweet Surrender

Dawn of Surrender

The MacKenzie World (read in any order)

Trouble Maker

Bullet Proof

Deep Trouble

Delta Rescue

Desire and Ice

Rush

Spies and Stilettos

Wicked Hot

Hot Witness

Avenged

Never Surrender

Stand Alone Titles

Breath of Fire

Kill Shot

Catch Me If You Can

All About Eve

Paradise Disguised

ALSO BY LOUIS SCOTT

Books by Liliana Hart and Scott Silverii

The Harley and Davidson Mystery Series

The Farmer's Slaughter

A Tisket a Casket

I Saw Mommy Killing Santa Claus

Get Your Murder Running

Deceased and Desist

Malice in Wonderland

Tequila Mockingbird

Gone With the Sin

ABOUT LILIANA HART

Liliana Hart is a New York Times, USAToday, and Publisher's Weekly bestselling author of more than sixty titles. After starting her first novel her freshman year of college, she immediately became addicted to writing and knew she'd found what she was meant to do with her life. She has no idea why she majored in music.

Since publishing in June 2011, Liliana has sold more than six-million books. All three of her series have made multiple appearances on the New York Times list.

Liliana can almost always be found at her computer writing, hauling five kids to various activities, or spending time with her husband. She calls Texas home.

If you enjoyed reading *this*, I would appreciate it if you would help others enjoy this book, too.

Lend it. This e-book is lending-enabled, so please, share it with a friend.

Recommend it. Please help other readers find this book by recommending it to friends, readers' groups and discussion boards.

Review it. Please tell other readers why you liked this book by reviewing. If you do write a review, please send me an email at lilianahartauthor@gmail.com, or visit me at http://www.lilianahart.com.

Connect with me online:
www.lilianahart.com
lilianahartauthor@gmail.com

facebook.com/LilianaHart

twitter.com/Liliana_Hart

instagram.com/LilianaHart

bookbub.com/authors/liliana-hart

ABOUT LOUIS SCOTT

Liliana's writing partner and husband, Scott blends over 25 years of heart-stopping policing Special Operations experience.

From deep in the heart of south Louisiana's Cajun Country, his action-packed writing style is seasoned by the Mardi Gras, hurricanes and crawfish étouffée.

Don't let the easy Creole smile fool you. The author served most of a highly decorated career in SOG buying dope, banging down doors, and busting bad guys.

Bringing characters to life based on those amazing experiences, Scott writes it like he lived it.

Lock and Load – Let's Roll.

Made in the USA
Middletown, DE
24 July 2021